Magic

BY Heart

Books by Amy Gordon

The Gorillas of Gill Park

Midnight Magic

Return to Gill Park

The Secret Life of a Boarding School Brat

When JFK Was My Father

Magic

BY Heart

BY AMY GORDON

ILLUSTRATED BY
ADAM
GUSTAVSON

Holiday House / New York

The publisher would like to thank Lena Burgos-Lafuente
of the Department of Spanish and Portuguese at New York University
for checking the Spanish words and grammar in this novel for accuracy.

Library of Congress Cataloging-in-Publication Data
Gordon, Amy, 1949–
Magic by heart / by Amy Gordon ; illustrated by Adam Gustavson.–1st. ed.
p. cm.
Summary: When Arietta and her magic cloak are kidnapped by a
lonely magician, her family, friends, and animals come together
to find a way to rescue her.
ISBN 978-0-8234-1995-1 (hardcover)
[1. Kidnapping–Fiction.   2. Magic–Fiction.   3. Friendship–Fiction.
4. Human-animal communication–Fiction.   5. Self-perception–Fiction.]
I. Title.
PZ7.G65Mag 2007
[Fic]–dc22
2006024890

For my family

Magic
BY Heart

Ten o'clock in the morning at the Mink Street Deli: There was always a little lull in the day, a time when Sam and Belle could stop working for a moment.

Belle stood sprinkling a little pastry flour on the counter and wrote names with her finger—Rosie, Lily, or Dahlia—names for a baby girl. A boy, though—he'd be company for Sam, and Belle pictured a strong, sturdy boy with a name like Stan or Sid.

Sam sat with a cup of coffee and the newspaper at a table by the window. He was only pretending to read the paper. He was really watching people go by—mothers pushing their babies in strollers, fathers teaching their little kids to ride bikes.

Sam and Belle were young and strong and happy in their work; you could get the best hot pastrami sandwich in the city at the Mink Street Deli. But still, there was sadness in Sam's and Belle's lives, for they longed with all their hearts for a baby girl or a baby boy. This good fortune had so far escaped them.

And then one day as Sam was sitting with his ten o'clock cup of coffee and staring out the window, he saw a giant pigeon swoop down and attack a small woman. It swirled above her head, darting for her eyes, her nose, her ears.

Without thinking, Sam rushed out the door. Although he was frightened—the pigeon

was the size of a Saint Bernard or a Great Dane—Sam waved his newspaper and stamped and shouted. Finally the giant pigeon flew away with a husky cry.

"*¡Qué horror!*" the small woman moaned. She dropped her bags. Papers, notebooks, pens, and pencils all went flying. Sam helped her pick them up, and Belle, too, who had rushed out as soon as she had seen all the commotion.

"Now I shall be even later than ever, but I thank you very much," said the woman. "If you had not come along, I would have been pecked to pieces. It is that nasty El Maloliente, the Evil One, who sends his smelly giant pigeons to attack me. Someday, I fear, they will get the better of me. But in the meantime, let me repay you for your kindness: I will grant you any wish you might have."

Sam and Belle looked at her in surprise.

The small woman patted her hair, trying to put it back in place. "I am Silvia Flores," she said. "I might look like I am just an ordinary Spanish teacher, but I am not so ordinary, you know. I am *una encantadora de comida*, an enchantress of food, and as you can see, I am young and beautiful, and that is why the Ugly One, the Hideous One, El Maléfico, has it in for me."

"But if you are a witch, can't you cast a spell on him, or on the pigeons he sends?" Belle asked.

"No, no," Silvia cried out. "I am not the abracadabra kind of witch. I am a food specialist. I use *ananás, pimientos, chirivía, salsa, sardinas, y sal*. Pineapples, peppers, parsnips, salsa, sardines, and salt," she quickly translated when she saw that Sam and Belle did not understand her. "And many other kinds of food, too. So what is it that you wish for?"

Sam and Belle first looked at each other, and then at the little teacher with a book bag in each hand, a bright scarf tied neatly around her neck. They looked at each other again. They did not really believe this woman could grant a wish, and yet each could read the longing in the other's heart.

"We wish for a child," Sam spoke for them both.

"A child! *¡Seguro!* Certainly!" Silvia nodded her head. "That one I have done before. Come with me."

She crossed the street to Luigi's Grocery, where the fruits and vegetables were piled high just outside the store. "*Alcachofas,*" she said, pointing to the artichokes. "You must put them in a pot and boil them. When they are tender, one by one you will pull off the leaves and dip the tips into a sauce. *Mantequilla y limón,* butter and lemon, or *vinagre y aceite.* Vinegar and oil. Béarnaise or hollandaise—these are nice, too. You dip, you scrape with your teeth, you taste! Until you reach the heart—and there you scrape away the thorny choke, and *delicioso!* Delicious! *¡Muy sabroso!* So tasty! As you eat the heart you make the wish of your heart. Every night for one year you must each eat one *alcachofa,* and you shall have that baby! And from each artichoke you must each save one leaf and dry it until it becomes as soft as silk. This is *muy muy importante*—very very important—and now I must go. I am late to my class, and my students will be raising the roof. *Buena suerte y muchas gracias por todo.* Good luck and thank you for everything. I shall see you again when you are holding that baby in your arms. I shall be the godmother, the *madrina.*"

And with that, Silvia marched briskly off down the street and disappeared as she turned right on the corner of Mink and 21st.

2

His real name was Héctor, but his sister, Silvia, called him all sorts of other names like El Malhechor, El Maléfico, El Malicioso, El Malhumorado. *Mal* is a prefix meaning "bad," and bad is what she thought her brother was. Big, muscular, attacking pigeons—that was Héctor's kind of magic all right!

But why was Silvia so sure it was Héctor?

At a young age Héctor had learned enlarging and shrinking magic from Abuelito, their

grandfather. It was magic that involved chocolates and peanuts, not at all difficult—magic
for beginners, for children—but Héctor had
never outgrown his delight in these kinds of
tricks. He still liked enlarging frogs and letting them loose in people's beds.

So as it turned out, Silvia was absolutely
right about Héctor and the pigeons. One day
he had been sitting in the park indulging in
his predilection for chocolate, when a group
of pigeons came crowding around, the way
pigeons do, looking for treats. Héctor tossed
them a crumb of chocolate, amusing himself
by uttering the magic charm to make them
grow. It was a satisfying charm. It only took a
few moments to take effect.

Soon Héctor amused himself even more by
enlarging a whole flock. Then he decided it
would be fun to torment his sister, Silvia, by
sending a giant pigeon after her. She always
had been a Goody Two-shoes, the brainy one in

the family, and the one, too, who had gotten all the good looks. It wasn't fair for her to be so beautiful when he was so ugly.

Ah, poor Héctor, he wasn't really ugly, but he had started to think so on his seventh birthday, on the day of the big fight between his father and his grandparents. It wasn't the first fight, but it was the worst.

"There will be no more magic in this house!" Pepe, his father, had shouted at *Abuelito* and *Abuelita,* the grandparents who lived with them. Poor, big, kind Abuelito and lively, little Abuelita. Why, Héctor wondered, was his father always shouting at them? It didn't make sense.

"Magic is part of our grandchildren's heritage!" Abuelito shouted back. Héctor didn't know what the word *heritage* meant, but it sounded important. "We come from a long line of magicians! Our daughter, your own wife, is a magician! We had hoped our grandchildren would carry on the family traditions."

"Well, I am not a magician, and I don't want my children to be, either," Pepe retorted angrily.

"I knew it!" Abuelita snapped. "Our María should have married a magician instead of, instead of . . ." Abuelita's voice trembled and she could not finish the sentence. Héctor knew, somehow, that she should not have begun the sentence. There was silence for a moment.

But then Pepe said, "You must both leave my house at once." He said it in an ice-cold voice, and Héctor felt himself shiver. "You cannot stay under this roof a moment longer. We have asked you many times not to teach the children magic, not to talk about it, not to practice it, and you persist in going against our wishes. Only just today, on Héctor's birthday, you were trying to teach him magic. This cannot go on any longer! You are a bad influence!"

"A bad influence!" Abuelito and Abuelita cried out.

The word *bad* jumped into Héctor's ears and burned all through him from head to foot, as if he had eaten a hot, hot pimento. He could scarcely breathe. How frightening his father sounded when he used that word—*bad*. Yes, that's what he, Héctor, was for using magic when his parents were always telling him not to. And now his grandparents were in trouble because of him.

A few moments later Abuelito and Abuelita came and held him, tears running down their faces. They packed their bags and left the house.

The house felt so empty, sad, and quiet. Abuelita had kept birds, colorful parrots and parakeets, and now they were all gone. Abuelito had always smelled of the chocolates and peanuts he carried in his pockets; now the house just smelled of furniture polish.

Finding Héctor standing alone in the hallway, his father said, "*¡Ay, qué feo!* How ugly you look, Héctor. What an ugly little face you are making."

The words bounced into Héctor's ears and sank like a stone into his heart. He happened, at that moment, to be facing the hall mirror. He looked into it. *¡Qué feo!* Yes, how ugly he was. His father was right. He *was* ugly!

In a matter of moments Héctor, on his seventh birthday, felt himself turn into a little island of ugliness. And from then on, if you approached him, you had a feeling that dangerous sharks were swimming all around him. And that was the day, also, that Héctor and Silvia began not to get along with each other.

3

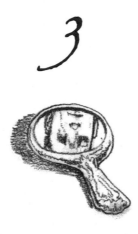

Héctor lived about a hundred blocks north of Sam and Belle in a castle that was really a museum for medieval artifacts, like suits of armor and swords and battle-axes and large carved wooden chests and tapestries. By day Héctor was a guard. By night he was supposed to leave the Castle. But he didn't. He secretly lived there, sleeping in one of the rooms that was closed to the public.

You might wonder if it is boring to be a guard in a museum, but Héctor was never bored, because his mind was always occupied. He would think about how ugly he was, how jealous he was of his sister, how mad he was at his parents for sending his beloved grandparents away. He was so mad at his parents, he hadn't seen his parents in years; in fact, no one in his family had any idea of where he was living.

As a guard, Héctor spent a lot of time staring at people, wishing he looked like this person or that. And then one night he made an extraordinary discovery.

He happened to be poking through one of the old chests in one of the rooms. He found a small, ornate hand mirror that had perhaps belonged to a fair damsel a long time ago. Most of the time Héctor never, never looked into mirrors, because it depressed him so much. But this time, before he could stop himself, he found himself gazing into the little looking glass. As usual, his own image made him want to stick out his tongue at himself. He quickly set it aside. But it was a pretty little thing, that mirror.

Héctor picked it up again, not to look into, but to study more closely. That was when he discovered his image was still in the glass *even though he wasn't looking into it.* His own face was staring back at him, sort of the way a fried egg can look up at you from the frying pan. And what's more, he discovered the mirror could keep his image in the glass for six whole hours before it disappeared.

The next day, out of curiosity, Héctor held the little looking glass up to visitors to the museum. Sure enough, other people's images could be captured, and that's how Héctor made another discovery. He had asked a beautiful woman to look in the glass, and now he was gazing admiringly at it. A few moments later, just by chance, he walked by an ordinary mirror that hung in one of the hallways. Usually he averted his eyes as he walked by, but this time he caught a glimpse of . . . the beautiful woman! His own horrible, repulsive features had been replaced by her beautiful ones!

Héctor was able to keep this new, wonderful face on for six hours—that is, for one half of a day. Amazingly, the face could smile or frown, look thoughtful or surprised, yawn, bite its lip, blink its eyes, and sneeze, plus all the other thousand things faces can do.

What a temptation for someone who thought he was ugly! From then on Héctor always carried the looking glass with him, and when he saw someone he thought was especially handsome or beautiful, he held up the glass and shouted, "Look!" That way he could wear the face of a man *or* a woman, sometimes even a child. He could be as young or old as he liked. He could be any color, too.

You'd think being able to look any way he wanted would make Héctor cheer up and stop thinking bad thoughts. But it didn't—partly because he knew he wasn't wearing his real face, but partly because people would often come up to him and mistake him for someone they knew. They thought he was their husband or wife or mother or best friend or tax accountant.

Wearing someone else's face can be awkward and embarrassing.

4

A year went by. Sam and Belle ate many artichokes. At first they ate them, leaf by leaf,
with a vinaigrette of oil and vinegar, mustard,
and garlic. But being artists with food, they
gradually grew more creative. They tried different recipes—stuffed artichokes with mush-
rooms, with shrimp, with veal, with lamb. But
no matter what, each time they came to the
heart, within their own hearts they made
their wish.

Luckily, Sam and Belle never tired of the taste of artichokes. And they were always careful to each save one leaf, hanging it to dry from the ceiling of their shop, until decorative garlands hung above the heads of their customers.

In a year Belle knew at last she was going to have a child.

And true to her word, Silvia appeared on the joyous day the baby was born. The baby was a girl, with black hair and dark eyes. Sam and Belle fell instantly and deliciously in love with her.

What did they name her? For years and years Sam and Belle had thought of names for a child, but Silvia now told them, as the baby's *madrina,* her godmother, she would like the honor of naming her. Sam and Belle thought that was the least they could do.

"In six months," Silvia said, "I shall return for the Naming Celebration," and with that she left, taking all the silky artichoke leaves with her.

For six months Sam and Belle simply called their baby, Baby Dove, or Lambkins, or Little Darling, or one hundred other sweet names, until the day for naming finally came.

Sam and Belle held the Naming Celebration in the evening. Having closed the deli all day in order to cook and bake, they finally opened the doors wide. Friends and family from far and wide poured in, among them many of the shop owners on Mink Street—the Changs, of course, who ran the Smiling Dragon Restaurant across the street; and Pinela and Luigi Morella, of Luigi's Market; Ivan, the owner of the secondhand bookstore; and Mr. and Mrs. Mann (Mr. Mann made grandfather clocks and music boxes in his shop just down the street). Belle's Aunt Sadie and Uncle Walter even made the trip from across the river.

And oh, the food! Besides little sandwiches of all kinds, Sam and Belle served three-bean salad and sautéed sea squab. The desserts were out of this world; never had Sam and Belle baked so many different kinds of cakes—cheese and carrot, cherry and chocolate, rum-banana-walnut, lemon-vanilla. There were apple pies and pecan pies, rhubarb, strawberry, and blueberry. The cream cheese brownies were to die for. And the raspberry tarts—they melted in your mouth!

It just so happened that Héctor was downtown, out and about that evening. As he approached the deli he saw the bright lights and all the people. He smelled the coffee and the delicious food wafting out the door. The creamy fudge frosting on the lemon-vanilla cake had a definite come-hither look about it. Héctor could never resist chocolate.

Earlier in the day Héctor had taken the

face of a striking middle-aged man, so now he felt handsome and confident, and he thought there would be no harm in stepping into that brightly lit deli and mingling with all the people. Lucky for him, too, Aunt Sadie lunged toward him, thinking she recognized him.

"Oh, Anton Van Lennep, the famous fashion designer, is here," she said, pulling him right into a cluster of people. "I just love your work," she gushed into his ear.

"I hope someday to be able to buy one of your evening gowns," a pretty woman said. Héctor began to feel happy. He liked pretty women, but he didn't often feel comfortable speaking to them. Helping himself to a piece of cake, Héctor reveled in all the attention he was getting.

Sam tapped a glass. Belle stood beside him, holding the baby in her arms.

"Hello, everybody," he said when the room

had quieted down. "Belle and I couldn't be happier or more proud to celebrate the arrival of our baby."

Everyone cheered and applauded.

"And we are pleased so many of you could be here on this exciting occasion. I now would like to introduce you to a special person. Standing next to me is the guest of honor, Silvia Flores, the godmother of our baby. Tonight she is going to give our precious, adorable child a name!"

Everyone cheered again, except for Héctor, who had not known his sister was in the crowd. He looked around, hoping to escape—he certainly didn't want to stay at a party where she was the guest of honor. But too many people were standing in his way for him to move, and Silvia was already tapping another glass for silence.

"And now," Silvia said, taking the baby from Belle and holding her up. "I shall give this child a name befitting a queen, for a queen she is in every way. She shall be called *Arietta de las Alcachofas,* or, in English, Arietta of the Artichokes."

"Ohhh," a ripple of enthusiasm went through the room.

"But she may be called just plain Arietta."

"Arietta," everyone in the room repeated.

"Or Arie is also acceptable."

"Arie," everyone cooed.

"A gift of the artichokes she is," Silvia went on in a slightly hushed tone of voice, "and a gift she was born with . . ." She paused for a moment and everyone leaned in. "She has the gift to see into the hearts of all the people around her."

"Ohhhh," said everyone in the room again, and the words *gift* and *hearts* were repeated over and over as people looked first at Silvia and then at Arietta with respect and awe.

5

"Come see Arietta of the Artichokes," one of Héctor's admirers said to him. Héctor was pushed into the center of the room. He found himself standing next to his sister, who was holding the baby. "Oh, Anton, you made it!" said Silvia enthusiastically. "I was so hoping you'd accept my invitation!"

"Oh!" said Héctor, not quite knowing what to say. He felt prickly having to stand next to his sister, of all people, and now it

seemed she had even invited the man whose face he was wearing.

Silvia was beaming at him. "I asked you to come because I knew once you met Arietta, you could not refuse to make one of your magical cloaks for her. She is enchanting, is she not?" Before Héctor could answer, Silvia handed him Arietta to hold.

It was at this moment that the real Anton Van Lennep arrived. The deli was so crowded, no one noticed that two men who looked exactly alike were standing in the same room. Of course, they weren't wearing the same clothes. Even though it was a warm summer night, Héctor was sweating it out in a long black coat and scarf and gloves (which he always carried with him for reasons you will shortly understand). Anton Van Lennep was black and Héctor was white; naturally, Héctor did not want his white neck and white hands to show. Anton, lucky fellow, was looking very cool and casual in a light blue cotton shirt and white linen pants.

The real Anton Van Lennep made his way to the center of the room. It wasn't very long before Anton and Héctor were standing side by side.

Anton looked at Héctor, and Héctor looked at Anton.

"Why, Anton," said Silvia, looking at them in astonishment, "I never knew you had a twin brother."

"I never knew I did, either," Anton said in great surprise.

Héctor had been having such a good time, he hadn't paid attention to how many hours had gone by. Right at this moment, before every-one's eyes, his face began to change. The lovely darkness drained out of his skin. The long, shapely nose became smaller and less distinguished. The full mouth became somewhat thinner. The long gray hair became short and dark.

"Ooh," everyone said, shrinking back in fear and surprise, everyone, that is, except Arietta, who, gazing up at the new face, broke into a big smile.

"Héctor!" Silvia exclaimed.

But Héctor wasn't paying attention. He was looking at Arietta, into her dark eyes, at her smiling face. He was experiencing shock. This little baby was looking up at him in such a trusting way. This little baby didn't care if he was ugly!

Héctor knew in that moment that what he needed in his life was a child. Maybe this little girl? But no, what was he thinking? This child belonged to someone else. What did he have to do to get his own child? He needed a wife, but who would marry someone as ugly as he was?

Just minutes ago the women had been swarming around him. Well, he would just keep on using Anton Van Lennep's face, and before long someone would surely want to be with him. But if he was always wearing Anton Van Lennep's face, he'd never be able to take his clothes off, and that would make everything very difficult.

All these thoughts flashed in a matter of seconds through Héctor's mind, but now he looked around wildly as he became aware of the commotion around him. His sister was screaming. The real Anton seemed to be yelling. Taking one last look at the smiling Arietta, he thrust her into Silvia's arms and ran out into the street. He darted, panic-stricken, through the throngs of people. Would the crowd in the deli follow him? Could he be put in jail for stealing another man's face?

Ducking into a back alley, Héctor paused to catch his breath. A row of pigeons sleeping in the eaves above him caught his eye. He chucked a loose piece of curb at them. As a pigeon drowsily fluttered down, Héctor held out a piece of chocolate he always carried with him. The pigeon pecked at it, and Héctor muttered a charm. It was the same charm he had learned many years ago from Abuelito, and in a few moments the pigeon began to grow. Héctor nibbled on a packet of peanuts he always kept for emergencies. Muttering a different charm, he shrank a little, just small enough so that clambering onto the back of the giant pigeon was no problem.

Héctor and his pigeon flew up and away, over the city to the Castle, where no one knew he lived. An hour or so later, when the shrinking charm had worn off and he was back to his regular size, Héctor thought once again of Arietta and how she had smiled in that moment his true face had been revealed.

6

Arietta brightened the days for Sam and Belle. How they loved the look of her—that black curly hair; that button nose; those rosy cheeks; those deep, dark eyes—and she was no trouble, no trouble at all. As she grew, she was perfectly content playing by herself in a corner of the deli or standing by her mother and father's side helping them—pouring flour into a bowl or frosting cupcakes—or sitting in Ivan the bookseller's lap as he taught her to read. She fed the Changs' black-and-white cat, Xiaolu, tidbits from the deli or sat listening, entranced, to one of Mr. Mann's music boxes.

But not all people were at ease around Arietta. If anyone had asked, they might have agreed that Arietta was pretty, but those deep, dark eyes—sometimes they were afraid to look at her, for when she looked back at them, that's when their insides gave a little twist. They remembered then the gift Silvia Flores had said Arietta was born with—the gift for seeing into the hearts of people. Yes, she seemed to see straight into their hearts and to see things that maybe they did not want anyone to see.

There was, for instance, Max, a handyman who came in to build new shelves for Sam and Belle. He winked at Arietta when he first entered the deli—she was sitting at a table playing with her dolls, but she stared at him for one long minute, at his wide, jolly face and puppy-dog eyes, and then turned away. Max's heart gave a little twist.

Still, all that day Max whistled cheerfully while he worked, and sang, and told jokes to Sam and Belle. They laughed and laughed, but Arietta refused to laugh and sat frowning more and more.

"What is the matter with you today?" Sam asked Arietta when Max finally finished the job and left.

"That's not a funny man," she said.

"Oh, Arie, Arie," said Sam, giving her a kiss on her cheek, "Where is your sense of humor?"

But the next moment there was a screech from Belle. She flew out from behind the counter. "Our money!" she cried. "Our money's gone!" And sure enough, all the money had been taken from the till. Sam and Belle had no idea where Max lived nor how to find him. And what was even worse, the shelves he had made were all crooked. Anything you put on them just rolled right off and fell to the floor.

"You were right, Arie," Sam said, shaking his head in wonder.

"How did you know?" asked Belle, flustered.

"You should not be surprised," said Silvia, who had just arrived and had been told the story. "She is, after all, *Arietta de las Alcachofas!*"

Héctor, meanwhile, was at that very moment on his way to the deli. It was important to him to see how Arietta was faring as she grew up, so he came to the deli once a week.

Every time he came, he was careful to wear a different face and not stay too long. What if the face he was wearing dissolved again? He didn't think he could bear the pain and shame of it. Besides, his sister, Silvia, was there far too often, at least every other time he came to visit.

But now as he made his way toward the deli he hadn't chosen a face to put on yet. Impulsively, he stopped and flashed the magic looking glass at someone he saw walking toward him—in rather a hurry, he thought, but he was glad he managed to catch the face; there was something about it that made him happy. As he put it on, Héctor felt himself grow jolly inside. He was actually grinning from ear to ear as he stepped into the Mink Street Deli.

And there was Arietta, sitting at the table next to her father—but who was sitting on her other side? *Ay, no,* it was his sister again, that interfering witch! *¡Ay, no! ¡Qué horror!* What was happening now? Sam was standing up and shaking his fist and shouting. Belle had come out from behind the counter with her rolling pin and was brandishing it at him.

7

"It's you, is it?" Belle shouted. "You no good louse. You thief in a carpenter's apron, pretending to hammer and saw and make us new shelves. How dare you show your face in here?"

"I'm locking the door. Someone call the police!" Sam ran to the deli door.

"No, no, Mama, Papa!" Arietta was looking at Héctor very closely. "It's not the same man! That's not Max."

"What do you mean, Arietta?" Sam asked, standing with his arms folded, glaring at Héctor, who, poor fellow, had borrowed the face of the handyman thief. He really was unlucky. With millions of faces to choose from, here he had gone and found exactly the wrong one!

"He looks like the same man, but he isn't—he's different." Arietta went over to Héctor and took him by the hand.

"Look at that," said Belle in amazement. "She wouldn't even so much as give him a smile when he was here before."

"She sees something we can't see," said Sam, slowly moving away from the door.

"¡Ay, verdad!" Silvia exclaimed. "Of course. We must listen to her."

"But he looks so much like the other one," said Sam, taking a step closer to Héctor in order to get a better look.

"He likes chocolate cupcakes," said Arietta. "Don't you?" she asked, tugging on his arm.

Héctor nodded, afraid to speak, afraid that his sister would recognize his voice. Unfortunately, when he put on other people's faces, their voices didn't come with the rest of the package.

"And he can fix the shelves."

It was true. Arietta had looked into his heart and had seen that Héctor liked building things. On that awful day when his grandparents had left in such a hurry, he had gone downstairs into the basement and had begun making birdhouses. Day after day all through his childhood he had made them—simple ones with just one opening and big ones where whole flocks could nest. Abuelita had so loved all kinds of birds. He had hoped that if he made enough birdhouses and birds came to live in them, Abuelita would come back and live with them again, too. In the process Héctor had become very handy.

So when Arietta led him back behind the counter to look at the crooked shelves, he knew just what to do. In no time at all, every shelf was as right as rain. Not a single jar or bowl or cup rolled one little inch.

"Now we'll give him a chocolate cupcake," said Arietta, skipping about. "His favorite thing."

"He could be that other man's twin," Belle said, shaking her head as Héctor sat down at the table by the window and Arietta brought him a cupcake. "But he builds very good shelves."

"*Sí, es verdad,*" said Silvia thoughtfully. "It's true." But an odd thing was happening to Silvia as she looked at the man with the puppy-dog eyes and the wide, jolly face. Certain words she had just heard were swimming inside her head. The word *chocolate,* for intance, was wriggling this way and that—oh yes, *chocolate,* that was her brother's favorite thing. And *twin*—how the word frisked about in between her ears, knocking against her brain, trying to remind her of something.

Finally, Silvia remembered another time she had stood right inside this delicatessen, yes, right here, on this very spot. It was at Arietta's Naming Celebration, and she had been talking to Anton Van Lennep when another man with the exact same handsome face had come and stood next to him. She had said, "You must be twins," and just as she had said that—*poof!* one of the men's faces had shivered and shimmered and dried up like a puddle on a very hot day. The face that was left was the face of Héctor, that very bad brother of hers.

Brothers and sisters, because they have grown up together under the same roof for so many years, because they have so much of the same blood running in their veins, sometimes can almost hear what the other is thinking.

That is what happened now. The words *chocolate* and *twin* and *bad brother* echoed in Héctor's ears. He hunched his shoulders.

Oh, Silvia knew those shoulders—yes, and she knew that hunch, all right. Hadn't she seen those shoulders hunch like that a million times before? Maybe he was wearing a wide, jolly face, but those shoulders, she'd have known them anywhere.

"Héc—" she started to say, but before she could say "tor," he had leaped from the table and bolted out the door, which Sam had never actually locked.

"Oh my," Silvia said to herself as she sat down at the table with a big sigh.

And that was all Silvia said on the subject, but she wasn't much fun for the rest of the afternoon. She was troubled. Arietta had said Héctor was a *good* man! Perhaps the child's gift for seeing into hearts was not mature yet. Some people she could see, and others not.

Silvia found herself wishing Anton Van Lennep would hurry up and finish the magic cloak he was making for Arietta, for she knew the cloak would help protect the child. But there was no hurrying the man—a Van Lennep cloak could take years to finish; in fact, it *was* taking years, and there was nothing she, Silvia, a Spanish teacher and a simple food enchantress, could do about it.

From then on, Silvia kept a close eye on Arietta. She made sure she explained the nature of her gift and where it had come from. She told Arietta that artichoke leaves had been saved by her parents and were being made into a marvelous magic cloak by a very famous designer; it would take many years for it to be finished, Silvia told her, as it could only be worked on nights when the moon was full and music was playing. And as the famous designer was always very busy, he was not always available to work on it.

"When will I get it?" Arietta wanted to know.

"On one of your birthdays," Silvia told her, "but even I do not know which one."

Of course, each birthday that came along, Arietta could hardly sleep the night before. But so far, the marvelous cloak just remained an idea, a story, a promise, a dream.

Héctor continued to come into the deli every week, wearing a different face every time. Arietta, recognizing him, thought he was just playing an amusing game with her. He read stories out loud to her (wearing a face that easily could have belonged to a kindergarten teacher). He told her funny stories (wearing a nice, twinkly face) and made her laugh. For her part she found she could tell him things, like when she was feeling sad or mad, and she looked forward to his visits.

And as time went by, Héctor's life slowly changed. At the museum he was becoming more of a guide than a guard. He always took the time to explain what the exhibits were to the children who came to visit. He always imagined it was Arie he was talking to, and therefore, it was important to do the best job possible.

When Arietta was old enough to go to school, the school bully, who always teased and tormented the smallest children, left her alone. He was afraid of her dark, all-seeing eyes. The girls in her class were sometimes mean, but they were never mean to her. They felt she knew too much about them. The class clown never joked in front of her, and the class liar never told a tale when she was around.

As Arietta and her classmates grew older, if a teacher left the room, Arietta was put in charge. Surprisingly, the kids never minded this at all; in fact, sometimes they preferred Arietta to the teacher because she was always fair.

But Arietta sometimes minded. It wasn't always easy to be able to see into the hearts of other people. It wasn't always fun to be the one in charge, or the one who was always fair. Sometimes she wished she could just look at a person's face and not have the responsibility of knowing so much. She couldn't bring herself to gossip with the others, or gang up on another child, or even have one friend who was special.

But in fifth grade a new boy came into Arietta's class. His name was Gus. As Arietta looked into his heart she thought it was a little like his desk at school—messy, and full of interesting things, but with no malice in it at all—and right away she wanted to be his friend.

Gus was the first classmate Arietta had ever invited home. Sam and Belle were so happy, they fed him all sorts of delightful things. He ate and ate, and when he could eat no more, he and Arietta went outside. Gus saw Xiaolu, the Changs' cat, and called out to her. *"Miaow,"* he said, sounding exactly like a cat.

"Miaow," Xiaolu answered. She ran across the street from the restaurant and rubbed up against Gus's legs.

Then Gus sat down on the front step of the Mink Street Deli and launched into a long conversation with Xiaolu.

"Can you really speak to cats?" Arietta asked him in amazement.

Gus explained to Arietta that he had spent his early years behind a Dumpster, where a family of orange cats had cared for him, bringing him food, curling up against him and keeping him warm when it was cold. Cattish had been his first language, although he'd never really developed it very well. He'd been about two years old when a social worker found him and delivered him to the orphanage; but naturally, Gus was very fond of cats and found every opportunity he could to keep up with their lives, and to speak Cattish when he could.

Because cats are night creatures, one of the ways Gus kept up with them was to meet them when it grew dark. He had learned to let himself out of the orphanage very quietly after everyone else was asleep. He went to the Dumpster and found the orange cats he still considered family. Sometimes he went out prowling with them.

When Gus confided all this to Arietta, she could hardly contain herself. "Oh, let me come and prowl with you sometime," she pleaded.

"All right," he said. "You can come tomorrow night because there's supposed to be a full moon, and prowling is best when the moon is full. I'll meow under your window so you'll know when to come out."

At about eleven o'clock the next night, Arietta, who had not been able to go to sleep out of sheer excitement, heard a loud meow. It was such a good meow, she wasn't sure if it was a cat or Gus, but when she poked her head out her window, she saw the top of Gus's head, with its mop of curly hair. (By an interesting coincidence, Gus's hair was a light orange, the same color as the cats' fur.)

Very quietly Arietta tiptoed down the back stairs—her family lived just above the deli—and let herself out the back door.

9

Arietta had hardly ever been outside this late before. How different Mink Street looked! The awnings were pulled down over the storefronts like eyelids closed tight for the night. Only a few cars passed by, but lots of cars were parked on both sides of the street, looking as if they, too, were fast asleep. The streetlamps cast pools of light, and the moon, full and bright, poked itself up past a tall building and bathed everything in a soft glow. As they crossed the street a large orange cat came bounding up to them.

"This is Uncle," Gus said, introducing the cat to Arietta. The orange cat nodded politely at Arietta and then meowed something to Gus. "He wants to take us to a special place," Gus translated. "Come on!" He took Arietta's hand, and they began to run, following the cat.

At first they ran down streets familiar to Arietta. They passed their school. It was strange to look up at the windows at night knowing all the classrooms were empty. The playground was full of shadows. Arietta was glad to be running, not walking, by it.

Not all the buildings were dark. Lights blazed here and there, and plenty of restaurants and cafés were still open, with people sitting outdoors at tables. Waiters stood in the doorways gazing at them as they ran by. Arietta worried. Wouldn't people wonder what they were up to, two kids running about so late? She hoped they wouldn't encounter any-one they knew.

Now Uncle turned down a street Arietta was sure she had never been on before. It was quieter and darker than other streets, with fewer buildings and no streetlamps. They stopped at a tall, tall hedge. The cat darted into the middle of it, and Gus and Arietta followed, wriggling after him through the latticework of scratchy twigs and branches.

As they came out into a courtyard formed on all sides by the tall hedge, Gus and Arietta could hardly believe their eyes and ears. Lively dance music came lilting through the open windows of a small house that stood in one corner. In the street it had been the middle of winter; here in the courtyard it seemed to be summer. Trees, growing up from little squares of earth, were in full leaf, and roses bloomed. On this side, the hedge was green and leafy, and filled with sweet-smelling white flowers.

More cats appeared, leaping over, through, and under the hedge until the courtyard was filled with every sort of imaginable cat, of every stripe and color. Under the full moon, with the scent of flowers in the air, the cats rose up on their hind legs and began to dance the samba, joyful and carefree.

And then quite suddenly, the music, still coming from the house, changed to something regal and weighty, something old and baroque.

The cats formed two lines, facing each other. Slowly, gracefully, they extended their left paws, then their right. They bowed and swished their tails all in one clean motion, perfectly in unison. Prancing forward, they met a partner in the middle. They rubbed noses, swished tails, bowed again, and then re-formed to make a circle. Round and round they went, heads held high, paws delicately placed.

The music ended, and somewhere a dog bayed. The cats, including Uncle, dispersed,

leaping in all directions, and disappeared through the hedge.

"I've always heard that cats dance under the full moon, and now I've seen them," said Gus, his eyes bright. "I wish I could dance with them."

"Couldn't you?" Arietta asked.

Gus shook his head sadly. "They consider me too human."

The music began again. Arietta recognized the piece. It was "The Moonlight Sonata," which Ivan, the bookseller, liked to play on his piano from time to time. It drifted out through the open windows of the house.

Curious, Gus and Arietta crept toward the house. The music poured out, louder as they grew closer. Standing on tiptoes, they peered into one of the open windows. They saw a large, open room, lit only by moonlight. They discerned a piano, grand and black, in one corner of the room. Seated at the white keys, playing with its head thrown back, its green eyes glowing, was a large yellow cat.

And now, to one side of the piano, they saw a tall man sitting in a chair, his gray head bent over something spread out on his lap and flowing down to the floor. Scarcely daring to breathe, Arietta craned her neck. Now she could see green leaves and recognized their distinctive shape. The fingers of the man's right hand grasped a needle. It glinted in the moonlight and danced and darted through the leaves, now up, now down, in time to the music.

"It's a cloak," Arietta whispered, "A cloak of artichoke leaves." She watched in wonder—could it be hers? She remembered Silvia said it could only be worked on under a full moon while music was playing. A shiver ran down her back. The man seemed very intent on his task, and solemn. She knew, suddenly, that he must not be disturbed. Pulling Gus by the arm, she whispered, "Let's go."

10

The next night Arietta dreamed of the cloak. She dreamed it was wrapped around her, covering her from head to foot. It had a hood, which she could pull down almost over her eyes. The silky leaves felt warm and smooth and soft around her ears. And then artichoke leaves swirled about her, lifting her up and up. She was flying!

Arietta awoke with a deep longing for the dream to come true. She wanted to know if she would be able to fly when she had her cloak, but she couldn't quite bring herself to ask. Even though Silvia was a witch, Arietta had seen for a long time that three quarters of her godmother's heart was made up of "no nonsense." She was afraid to ask and have Silvia snap at her and say, "Of course not!" As long as she didn't know, Arietta could still imagine, and hope.

But Arietta and Gus were full of curiosity about the courtyard. What would it be like in daytime? Would it still be summer on the inside? Would the cat still be playing the piano?

But although she and Gus went looking that very afternoon after school, they were not able to find the hedge. They retraced their steps again and again, but it seemed to have completely vanished. Where they thought the hedge was supposed to be, they always encountered a high brick wall.

Gus soon learned from Uncle that the hedge could only be found when the moon was full, and only a cat could lead them through it. That meant waiting a whole month before they could go again.

Arietta was busy, though, and the days passed quickly, for she was planning a party to celebrate her tenth birthday. She had decided to invite all her classmates, and her friends who owned the shops on Mink Street. She was thrilled the day Héctor came in wearing the face of a young boy. She handed him an invitation, and no one guessed that he wasn't just one of her classmates at school.

The time passed pleasantly, too, because Gus and Xiaolu were trying to teach Arietta Cattish. Gus, to be sure, was not fluent in Cattish himself—he had, after all, been only two when he had been taken away from the cats.

He enjoyed improving his vocabulary, sitting every afternoon for about an hour right outside the deli with Arietta and Xiaolu. Arietta was coming along. She could now talk about the weather and say things like, "I like to eat salmon and liver."

So the days flew by, and once more on the night the moon was supposed to be full, Gus meowed beneath Arietta's window. Arietta quietly let herself out of the deli only to look up and see it was overcast and the moon was sometimes hidden by the clouds.

And this time the cats were preoccupied. Something strange was happening in the neighborhood—many of the pigeons were moving out, no one knew to where. It was unsettling, as if the balance of things had become disturbed. The squirrels didn't like it, either, and the cats and squirrels were getting together to discuss what, if anything, they could do about it. (Most city squirrels and cats speak a little of each other's language, and many, for that matter, also know a bit of human speech.) No one was available to lead Gus and Arietta to the courtyard.

"Maybe I sort of count as a cat," said Gus. "Let's try it, anyway."

Gus and Arietta set out, traveling the route they knew quite well now, past the school and cafés and restaurants, and then down the dark and quiet street. The moon at that moment emerged from behind a cloud, and there, miraculously, was the hedge.

"Come on," said Gus, but just as they were about to scramble through, there was the sound of shattering glass. A woman screamed and a man shouted. Turning around, Gus and Arietta saw a small woman kneeling on the pavement, wailing, "*¡Ay!* My mirror! My precious mirror!" A man was holding another man by the shoulders, shaking him and shouting, "You clumsy oaf! Why don't you watch where you're going? See what you've done!"

Arietta and Gus, ducking behind a tree, stood and watched. Arietta was surprised to recognize the man who was being shaken. It was Max, the handyman. She hadn't seen him in a few years, but even in the moonlight there was no mistaking his face, although at this moment it was more indignant than jolly.

"*You* bumped into *me! I* didn't bump into *you!*" Max exclaimed.

"What are you talking about?" the other man shouted.

"Let him go, Pepe," the little woman said sadly. "There is no use crying over broken glass. There is nothing we can do now."

"All right, María, all right, but a whole year's worth of work—a whole year—down the drain because of this clumsy oaf."

The man called Pepe slowly let go of Max, but Max, surprisingly, did not run off. As if in a trance, he bent down and picked up the broken mirror. He held it up by the handle and peered intently into what was left of it. Although some of the glass had fallen out, there was a large piece still in the frame.

"What is this?" Max asked. "What's happening?"

"What *is* happening?" María asked, taking a step near him and sounding very hopeful.

"I am seeing myself," said Max slowly. "But—well, a different side of myself than I usually see, a better side. I . . ." He stopped speaking for a minute, and then he handed the mirror carefully back to María. "I'm very sorry I bumped into you and broke your mirror," he said. "I bumped into you because I was going to pick your pocket. In fact, I did pick your pocket." He handed a wallet back to Pepe. "I've been a thief for a couple of years now, but I don't want to do that anymore. I hope you'll forgive me. I'll come and work for you, anything, to make amends."

María and Pepe looked at Max in astonishment, and Gus and Arietta, behind the tree, were also very surprised.

"It works!" Pepe exclaimed. "Even though the mirror is broken, the magic still works!"

"*¡Muchas gracias!*" María exclaimed, coming over and giving an astonished Max a kiss on the cheek. "*¡Usted es muy, muy simpático!* You are very, very nice! For a whole year I have been working on this, hoping to help my boy. I wasn't at all sure it was going to work, and I have been afraid to let anyone look into it. But now I'm going to make a new mirror, an even better one, and you can be the first to try it! Then I will know for sure I can help my son!"

"Here, take my card," said Pepe. "We live in the apartment building on the next block."

Max took the card and slowly, as if still in a trance, made his way down the street.

María stood in the street, a huge smile on her face. "Well, Pepe, what do you think of that?"

"Magic is marvelous," said Pepe, gazing fondly at his wife. "If only I had realized it sooner."

María put a hand on Pepe's arm. "Better late than never, *mi amor.*"

"But what we have to do now is keep looking for our boy before it *is* too late," said Pepe. "I wish we knew where he is living. This is such a big city, it is like looking for a needle in a haystack."

Arietta and Gus watched the couple walk away, arm in arm, down the street. They walked one block, and then turned into an apartment building. On a sudden impulse Arietta bent down and picked up one of the pieces of glass that had fallen out of the frame. It was a good size chunk and not too sharp. She carefully placed it in the pocket of her jacket. Maybe when she got home, she might just take a look. . . .

"Come on," said Gus. "Let's go through the hedge."

But the moon was hidden behind a cloud, and the hedge had vanished. It had begun to rain, and there was only a brick wall.

On the morning of her birthday, Arietta woke up early. She had dreamed about the cloak again, for the first time since that disappointing night when she and Gus had found the hedge and then had lost it again. She hugged herself, hoping that maybe today, when she turned ten, Silvia's gift would be the cloak.

Silvia came into Arietta's room early in the morning, but her present was not the cloak. It was a box of magic figs that Silvia said would keep Arietta's complexion smooth and acne free. A very nice present, to be sure, but Arietta found herself swallowing tears of disappointment. Still, she had her party to look forward to.

As Arietta hugged Silvia and thanked her, her eye was caught by the piece of glass she had picked up from the broken magic mirror. It had been sitting on top of her bureau all these days, and she hadn't been able to bring herself to look into it yet. Sometime today, though, on her birthday, she would. She carefully wrapped it in a piece of cloth and put it in her pocket, and then she went downstairs to the deli to help Sam and Belle get ready for the festivities.

Everyone Arietta invited came to the party—all her classmates, and her shop-owner friends on Mink Street. The Morellas brought Arietta ten of their largest artichokes. Ivan, the bookseller, gave her a lovely illustrated book of artichokes printed a hundred years ago. The Changs' gift was a lovely little vase shaped like an artichoke, and Mr. Mann's, a music box which played a delightful little tune called "The Artichoke Waltz."

Xiaolu even appeared and sang "Happy Birthday" to Arietta in Cattish. So everyone was there; everyone, that is, except for Héctor. Arietta looked around at all the assembled people and was sorry she did not see him.

There was so much delicious food and the kids were having so much fun—Arietta had never invited everyone in her class to the deli before—that she forgot all about the cloak.

After lunch the tables and chairs were pushed to one side. In the middle of the room, Silvia hung up a giant artichoke piñata, which she had made herself out of papier-mâché. She tied a blindfold around Arietta's eyes and handed her a stick. "Here, Arie," she said, "you be the first to try."

Every child had a turn, but in the first round no one managed to break open the piñata. The artichoke swung back and forth, and everyone, including Arietta, was too excited to pay much attention to the large ten-year-old girl who shuffled awkwardly into the deli. She was wearing long braids tied at the ends with ribbons, and a long dress that came down to the floor.

It was Gus's turn now, his second try. Silvia tied the blindfold around his eyes. He held the stick with two hands as if he were holding a bat. He went at that piñata with a mighty thwack—but still the artichoke merely swung in the air.

"Can I have a turn?" asked the new girl in a rather hoarse voice.

"Oh!" Arietta exclaimed, jumping up and down and clapping when she recognized Héctor. "You did come!"

"You come right over here," Silvia said gently. She prided herself on being good with shy children but she had a hard time getting the blindfold around the girl's large head, especially as the girl seemed awfully squirmy. At last it was tied.

The big girl reached up with the stick and *thwhack!* The papier-mâché artichoke cracked wide open.

All the children started screaming and jumping and pushing and lunging as candy poured out of the piñata and scattered all over the floor. No one saw the tip of a green leaf poke tentatively out of the hole—first one leaf and then another, until a mass of green leaves wriggled all the way out and swirled in the air above everyone's heads. It zoomed this way and that as if looking for something, and then, with a little shake, headed for Arietta.

The leaves cloaked themselves around her, billowing and rustling and ruffling and settling, and finally a green leafy hood settled snugly on her head and against her face, almost covering her eyes.

Arietta was surprised, delighted, and entranced.

"Oooh," everyone exclaimed in admiration. Unfortunately, Héctor's "Oooh" was louder and deeper than everyone else's, even Luigi's, and he had a pretty robust voice.

Silvia's head snapped up. "Héctor!" she cried out angrily. She stamped her foot. *"¿Qué haces aquí?* What are you doing here? You are like a bad dream! Go away! You were not invited to this party!"

"Oooh!" everyone exclaimed again, this time in great fear, for Héctor, who was still holding the stick, began swinging it around. "I was *too* invited!" he shouted back. But he stopped shouting as he saw everyone staring at him, especially the kids. They were all frightened of him, he could see, even if he wasn't wearing his own face. Oh, what was the point, anyway, of coming here and thinking he could have fun at a birthday party like regular people?

Héctor dropped the stick and ran out of the Mink Street Deli.

12

"Wait!" Arietta cried. "Don't go! You don't have to leave!" She began to run after Héctor as fast as her legs would carry her.

The cloak was cumbersome; Arietta kept tripping. Luckily, Héctor had shrunk himself quite a bit in order to fit in with ten-year-olds. Arietta was able to keep sight of him until, finally, he came to a stop in a back street.

Catching her breath, Arietta watched in amazement as Héctor untied a large pigeon that had been tethered to a streetlamp. "Come, Pitter, we must fly," he crooned to the pigeon as he climbed on its back. (Fortunately for Héctor, most pigeons spoke a little English; in a pinch Héctor could also manage a little Pigeonish.) With a fluttering of wings, Pitter took off.

"Wait!" Arietta called out in a small, pitiful voice. "I want to come with you! Let me fly, cloak, let me fly!"

She stood flapping her arms, thinking she might lift off the ground, but unlike in her dreams when she wore the cloak, nothing happened. "Oh!" she cried, tears streaming down her cheeks, of what use was her marvelous cloak of artichoke leaves after all? It was just heavy, and it tripped her, and—and—she probably looked silly and stupid. She started to wrestle out of it, but as she did so, she felt a pain in her side.

Arietta had forgotten all about the piece of magic glass! Carefully reaching into her pocket, she pulled it out and held it in her hand. *This is as good a time as any,* she thought desperately. Peering into it, she could only see one eye at a time, but oddly, as she did so, she had the sensation of little pinpricks dancing across her forehead. With the pricks came a thought flickering into her mind: *I have the gift of seeing into people's hearts, but it doesn't make me like them any less—not usually, anyway.*

Arietta felt light and happy and proud—and it seemed to be just what the cloak was waiting for: Leaf by leaf it began to stir and rustle, and in a moment Arietta was lifted off the ground.

At first, Arietta could scarcely breathe. Squeezing her eyes shut, she pressed her arms tightly against her sides. But as the delicious air rushed past her face she began to breathe more easily. She spread her arms as if they were wings, and dared, finally, to open her

eyes and look down. Cars and buses and taxis clogged every street as far as she could see. She was moving twice as fast as the rush-hour traffic below, soaring above the city, free as a bird!

Now, if she could only find Héctor. Scanning the sky, she thought she could just make out Pitter's tail and Héctor's back. "Hurry, cloak, hurry!" she coaxed out loud, and sure enough, she picked up speed, and the leaves of the cloak streamed out behind her. Soon she had closed enough distance between herself and Héctor to feel confident she wouldn't lose him.

In any case, Pitter slowed down as the towers of the Castle came into view. Héctor had learned to approach the upper courtyard from the northwest when he was coming in for a landing, an angle that made it impossible for most visitors to the Castle to spot his comings and goings. Because of this, Pitter suddenly veered off course, heading away from the towers. Then he circled back, hovering for a moment above one of the upper courtyards before descending abruptly.

Arietta found herself fluttering down, down, down, as slowly and gently as dandelion fluff. As she landed, a group of large, cooing and clucking pigeons excitedly converged on her, nearly knocking her over. Héctor, dismounting his pigeon, looked at her in astonishment.

"Hello," she said, very pleased with herself. "I followed you. But what are you doing here?"

Héctor hastily ran his fingers across his hair and face. The braids were gone, and he could feel his own rather small nose. *¡Ay, no!* He was himself! But *¡qué cosa maravillosa!* What a marvelous thing! Arietta was smiling at him!

"I live here," he said.

"This is where you *live?* In the *Castle?*"

"Yes," Héctor said, feeling proud for the first time of where he lived.

Arietta pushed her way past the pigeons, flustered by all their cooing and billing and fussing. "Can I see it?"

"Yes, of course" said Héctor, still amazed that she had followed him, not to mention she'd followed him by flying! He pulled the dress up over his head and off, which was a relief, as he was rapidly growing back to his regular size, and the dress worn over his own clothes was beginning to choke him. "Follow me." Héctor led Arietta down the stairs to the main part of the museum.

"Before I go another step, I'd like to hang my cloak up, please." Arietta began to wriggle out of it. "It's very hard to walk in."

Héctor took the cloak, marveling at the smooth silkiness of it, the beauty of the tiny stitches. It certainly was a work of art! Carefully placing it in an old chest, he said, "It's almost closing time. When all the visitors are gone, I'll take you on a tour. And then," he added, nearly dancing with excitement, "we'll play hide-and-seek all over the Castle!"

Arietta jumped up and threw her arms around Héctor. "This is the best birthday ever!" she exclaimed, and Héctor felt his eyes fill up with tears.

The tour began in the Great Hall. At every corner a knight in a suit of armor rode on a horse. Glass cases were filled with swords and lances, and battle-axes lined the walls. Arietta loved the solid feel of the stone floor beneath her feet, the soaring of the arched ceilings above her.

As they went from room to room Héctor explained the stories in the tapestries and in the stained glass windows. He told tales of queens and princesses who had worn the necklaces and crowns that were in the display cases. He told her how knights were trained and how swords were made. What a good story-teller Héctor was, and how he enjoyed having Arietta there to tell stories of them to, just as he had always imagined.

"And now we'll play," said Héctor when the tour was finished. "I'll be *it* first." Arietta knew all along where she was going to hide. She'd spotted a small suit of armor Héctor used for school tours (he'd actually been pro-moted to school tour leader a week ago), and she was able to climb right into it. While she was waiting for Héctor to find her she imag-ined that she was a knight all those years ago. When it was Héctor's turn, it took her a long time to find him, but as she went from room to room she kept thinking how grand and thrilling the Castle was and how marvelous it would be to live here all the time.

By the time the game was finished, the setting sun came in through the stained glass windows, making all the colors glow for a lovely minute; but then as soon as the sun went down, the Castle became dark and shadowy. It felt creepy to Arietta. She wanted suddenly to go home. "Thank you very much for a very nice time," she said.

"What do you mean?" Héctor asked.

"I want to go home now," she said. For the first time, she realized her parents must be wondering where she had gone. They must be very worried! Now she was worried, too, and felt a knot in the pit of her stomach. "I must go quickly!"

"No, no, first you must dine with me!" Héctor exclaimed. "You must have a birthday banquet fit for a queen. You shall have artichokes, of course, and a birthday cake."

Finding some cushions for her to sit on and an illuminated manuscript to look at,

Héctor rushed down to the Castle cellar, where he kept his food supplies. How fortunate! He just happened to have artichokes on hand (he liked them very much himself) and the makings for a chocolate cake (he made one almost every week).

Entranced by the intricate drawings of flowers and birds and animals in the old manuscript and the promise of a banquet and a cake—she had, after all, left her party before the birthday cake had been brought out—Arietta quickly forgot she wanted to go home and how worried her parents must be.

And then the next thing she knew, Héctor led Arietta to a long, long table; placed a crown of emeralds and rubies on her head; and sat her down in a thronelike sort of chair. He lit candles (held in the claws of bronze lions) and served her artichokes and chocolate cake on pewter dishes.

Arietta looked exactly like a small queen at

her place at the head of the table. Héctor, sitting way down at the other end, couldn't stop smiling. He realized the whole time he had been with Arietta, he had worn his true face without giving one thought to how he looked. He hadn't felt this happy since the days his grandparents had lived with him so long ago.

"I *must* go home now," Arietta said when the last crumb of cake had been devoured. "But if it's all the same to you, I'd rather not fly by myself in the dark. Perhaps I could ride behind you on one of the pigeons?" When Héctor did not answer right away, she stood up from the table and said more firmly, "Bring me my cloak, please."

Héctor slumped in his chair, looking miserable. The day was over now. He did not know what else he could do to keep Arietta. "The cloak," he croaked. "I will go and fetch it."

He left the room and then, out in the dark hallway, began pacing. He couldn't let Arietta go. He knew without a doubt that once Silvia found out where Arietta had flown off to, she'd never be allowed to visit him again. Silvia thought he was bad through and through, and that was that.

Héctor came back into the room looking solemn. "I'm afraid I accidentally locked your cloak in the chest, and I've lost the key. And, I'm sorry to say, the pigeons don't like to fly at night."

Arietta stared at Héctor. She could see right into his heart, and what she found there surprised her. He was planning on not letting her leave! She placed her hands squarely on her hips. "Are you *kidding?*" she asked indignantly.

"Would you mind staying and playing with me, please, oh please, just one more day?" he pleaded. "We can go out on the grounds tomorrow and find a tree and build a tree house."

Arietta had always wanted to build a tree

house. It was terribly tempting. "I can come back tomorrow," she said.

"But your parents and Silvia, that god-mother of yours, might not let you," said Héctor, looking very forlorn.

Arietta thought this over. Silvia, she real-ized, had shouted out Héctor's name at the party. Silvia knew him somehow! And now it seemed as if Héctor knew Silvia. And then Arietta jumped up and clapped a hand to her mouth.

"Silvia is your *sister!*" she exclaimed. The resemblance was suddenly as clear as day! There it was, in the shape of his nose and his mouth, and now that she thought about it, they both crinkled their eyes in the same way when they smiled. She might have realized it sooner, but of course, she'd never had the opportunity of seeing Héctor's true face until now. She really ought to ask him why he did that face-changing stuff all the time.

"She *is* my sister," Héctor admitted with a sigh.

"Well, how come you never speak to her? Don't you like her?" Arietta asked, amazed.

"Huh!" Héctor exclaimed. "You just try having a sister sometime. They're bossy and think they know everything, and they always get their own way."

"You're jealous," Arietta scolded.

Héctor glowered, pulling his eyebrows down and his mouth into a tight little line.

"Why, Héctor, what an ugly expression!" Arietta exclaimed. "Don't look like that!"

Héctor quickly covered his face with his hands. What was he going to do? She was beginning to see that he was ugly, and soon she would begin to hate him. He'd have to go out and find a better face to put on soon.

"But if you're Silvia's brother, then of course I can stay," Arietta said, suddenly clapping her hands and jumping up and down.

Her eyes were shining now. "I'm sure she told Mama and Papa who you are, and they won't be worried at all." Arietta felt a huge sense of relief at the thought of this.

Astonished, Héctor uncovered his face. "But you must write your parents a note, and we'll send it by pigeon," he said, trying, now that Arietta was going to stay, to do the right thing. "They will enjoy getting a note from you."

Héctor raced up to the upper courtyard, where the pigeons roosted together at night. He woke up the whole lot of them, asking for a volunteer to go out into the night and deliver a message.

Pitter, a brave and intelligent pigeon, said he would go as long as his wife, Patter, could also go with him. Arietta wrote her note, and the two pigeons set out, proud to be going on such an important mission.

That night Arietta went to sleep in a large canopy bed in one of the tower rooms. Now she wished she had not stayed. She was scared in that dark room and in that big bed with its shadowy curtains. She became even more scared when she heard a rustling.

She sat straight up, heart racing, but then when she felt the light touch of a soft, silky leaf on her cheek, she let out a cry of recognition. "Oh, it's you," she said happily, as her cloak wrapped itself around her. "You found me! And tomorrow I'll play with Héctor for just a little while because I said I would, but then I'll fly away home."

Cloaked safely in artichoke leaves, Arietta fell fast asleep.

Sam and Belle had been frantic. They had looked everywhere for Arietta, up and down Mink Street and for blocks and blocks beyond. They'd alerted the police and sent them out in search of her.

Silvia was hopping mad. She had seen the way Arietta had run after Héctor. She was sure she was with that brother of hers, but she did not know where he lived.

And then Pitter and Patter arrived, a little breathlessly as they weren't used to night flying. Sam and Belle and Silvia were greatly alarmed when they saw the two large pigeons in front of the deli door. But the pigeons merely stood outside, looking shyly at their feet. Luckily, Belle noticed the message attached to one of Pitter's legs. She rushed out, untied it, and with shaking hands came back in and handed it to Sam.

"You read it, Sam," she said. "I can't bear to."

"*As you know, I am with Héctor, Silvia's brother,*" Sam read aloud in a trembling voice. "*He gave me artichokes and chocolate cake to eat so you see I am fine. I am sorry I went off without telling you but I am hoping Silvia told you and I am telling you now and I will be home tomorrow. Love and kisses, your little Arie.*"

Sam and Belle felt a little better; still, they wished they knew where Héctor lived. They did not sleep well and by morning were very tired. Silvia had stayed over, and now she helped them with the morning chores and the rush of morning customers. By ten o'clock they were all relieved to take a break. Belle and Silvia joined Sam as he sat down with the newspaper. "Listen to this," said Sam. "There's an article in here about the giant pigeons." He cleared his throat as he began to read. *"Over the years, more and more people have sighted giant pigeons. Where do they come from? No one seems to know. But a huge flock of them are now living in the upper courtyard of the Medieval Museum, also known as 'the Castle.' Visitors are startled, and somewhat intimidated, to come across them. For the most part the pigeons do not seem to be aggressive. It is, however, a curious phenomenon, and ornithologists are beginning to pay attention."*

"What a crazy thing!" Silvia cried out. The connection between Héctor and the large pigeons was not lost on her. "So that is where I bet you anything Héctor is living these days, at that Castle where the giant pigeons are. That would be just like him." She jumped to her feet. "I will go there and bring Arietta back myself."

Silvia took the Number 6 bus all the way uptown. It took over an hour, and she found herself becoming uncharacteristically nervous. What if Héctor had on a different face and she didn't recognize him? He would certainly recognize *her,* and then he would have the advantage. He might even order the whole flock of giant pigeons to attack her. She wished she had thought to wear a disguise. But even if she had, she never had been very good at disguises. Some people can only be themselves.

While she was pondering all these things an ancient-looking crone climbed onto the bus. Her face had as many wrinkles as there are people in the city. She wobbled up the aisle and tottered into the seat next to Silvia.

"I am going to the Castle," the old woman announced in a creaky voice. "I read in the paper today that large pigeons are flocking there. I want to see them with my own eyes and speak to them directly."

"Speak to them?" Silvia asked, surprised.

"I am a professor of Avish, the language of birds," the old woman said. "I speak over one hundred of the dialects, Pigeonish among them."

"How impressive," said Silvia, who spoke eighteen human languages and was proud of that.

"I've always known a smattering of bird languages," the old woman said, "but I began studying them seriously when I was eighty

years old. At that time I went to live in an aviary, and I'm very glad that I did. I have spoken with birds from all over the globe. The most fascinating was a rainbow lorikeet from northern Australia."

And now an idea occurred to Silvia. Meeting this old person who was fluent in Avish was such a stroke of good luck! "I am going to the Castle also," she said, "and I was wondering if perhaps you could do me a favor."

"Do you a favor?" the old woman asked, surprised. "Well, certainly, if I can," she added agreeably.

"A young girl who is the daughter of dear friends of mine has gone for a visit to the Castle, and I'm coming to collect her and take her home. But, well, this may sound rather silly, but I'm a little afraid of the person she's visiting, and I was wondering . . . what I'm asking is . . . could you find the girl? She is ten years old, and has dark curly hair and dark eyes, and her name is Arietta. Could you find her and ask her to meet me at the bus stop?"

"Of course I can," said the old lady. "But what a shame you are so afraid of the person she is visiting."

"Yes," said Silvia. "It is a shame. As far as I am concerned, he is a bad good-for-nothing! Oh, he won't harm *you* in any way, of course—just me. He has a sort of grudge against me, so I really can't thank you enough!"

The old woman clucked sympathetically, and then the two of them went on to speak of this and that, and the rest of the bus ride passed very quickly.

As the bus chugged up the steep approach to the Castle, Silvia glimpsed large birds wheeling above the towers. She felt a little catch in her throat. Were they hawks . . . or pigeons? Well, never mind, she thought, a castle is a magnificent sight under any circumstances.

The bus stopped, and a small shuttle bus was waiting to take people all the way up the hill to the Castle.

As they climbed out at the top Silvia thanked the old woman one more time. Watching her totter away, Silvia hoped she would be all right. She certainly was old and frail. And she realized, suddenly, she had never asked her name. How unlike her not to inquire. It just showed how unusually upset and distracted she was.

The old woman, whose name was Ula, made her way through the front entrance of the Castle. Noticing a museum guide, she approached him and asked him the way to the upper courtyard, which was where the newspaper article said the pigeons might be.

The guide, who was Héctor, was stunned by the face of the very old woman. Some people think only the young are beautiful, but Héctor was sensitive to beauty in all ages.

He thought Ula had very fine bone structure, and that her eyes had a lustrous shine.

It occurred to Héctor that if he wore this woman's face, Arietta surely would think he was kind and wise and wonderful. He'd had a bit of trouble with her earlier in the day. It was a shame, really, when for the most part, everything had gone so well.

He quickly held the mirror up to the old woman, and then before she could ask what he was doing, pointed her in the direction of the elevator that would lead to the upper courtyard.

"I would prefer the stairs," said Ula. "It is by never riding elevators that I have stayed young."

"Very well," said Héctor, full of admiration for her. He showed her the way.

Ula climbed the narrow, winding stairs to the upper courtyard. There she beheld the cluster of oversize pigeons. It wasn't long before she was deep in conversation with them.

The pigeons explained how they had grown larger when the Master of the Chocolate had fed them, and how much they enjoyed being this size, so they had chosen to come live at the Castle. They were intrigued to meet a human who could speak their language so well (she was, of course, much better at it than Héctor was), but when they discovered that Ula had met a great many of their cousins in Venice, Paris, and London, they were ecstatic.

She was about to ask them if they knew anything about a girl named Arietta when she noticed that every few minutes several of them flew up to a tower window and then back down again. She asked them what was up there.

"That's our fledgling," said Ruth, one of

the largest and bossiest of the pigeons. She had put herself in charge of the flock and made herself the spokesbird for them.

"Your fledgling?" Ula asked. "You have a nest in the tower?"

All the pigeons started chuckling softly.

"No, no, no, silly Ula," chuckled Ruth.

"Silly Ula, silly Ula, silly Ula," all the pigeons repeated.

"That's a human fledgling. Her name is Arietta."

"Arietta, Arietta, Arietta," murmured the pigeons.

"Arietta?" Ula asked, confused.

"She belongs to the Master of the Chocolate," said Ruth.

"Master," the pigeons all breathed the name like a long sigh. "Chocolate."

"It's feeding time," Ruth said, breaking into the chorus. "Who's on duty?"

Pitter and Patter stepped forward. "We are," they said.

"Something strange is going on here," Ula thought to herself. "Please, take me up to see her," she said out loud, making sure her coat was firmly buttoned and her collar up to keep the cold off her neck.

Now, Ula was almost one-hundred-and-one years old. She was extremely tiny and very light, so she was unlikely to be a burden to the pigeon. She was also an unusually brave person to climb on the back of a bird—it was Pitter—and wrap her arms around his neck and allow herself to be lifted off the ground.

At first she did not even shut her eyes but took in the great river unraveling like a silver thread below her. She saw its ships and barges, and where the ice had formed along the shore. She saw the great bridges, their intricate ironwork looking like cobwebs from this height, and the miles and miles of build-ings—how could human beings have built so much, she wondered—and somewhere down among those millions of people were people she had loved but lost somehow. How she had lost them, she wasn't really sure, but all at once she felt dizzy. She should not have been thinking about those people she had loved but lost. She shut her eyes. The earth was too far below, and she too high.

Pitter flew through the tower window—if he had been any larger, he would not have fit, for the windows were narrow—and landed near the bed Arietta was sitting on.

"Who are you?" Arietta asked, jumping up from the chest. "Have you come to rescue me?"

Héctor walked toward the bus stop. He was off duty now, and eager to go downtown wearing his new face, mingle with people, and then buy some more artichokes for Arietta. Arietta would surely cheer up if he fed her artichokes. She might even possibly stop being mad at him for locking her in the tower. Héctor was so busy thinking these thoughts that he did not see Silvia right away. He almost fainted from shock when she got up from a bench and walked right up to him.

"Oh, I am glad to see you!" she said. "I was getting cold just sitting here. Arietta hasn't come down to meet me yet. Did you have any luck finding her?"

It took Héctor a few panicky moments to realize that Silvia not only did not recognize him but somehow knew the person whose face he was wearing. As he pulled himself together, he was roughly able to connect the dots. Silvia must have sent the old lady to look for Arietta!

Trying as hard as he could to remember how the old lady's voice had sounded, Héctor said, "No, no, I'm afraid I did not find her. I'm so sorry."

"*¡Qué lástima!* What a shame!" said Silvia. "Well, unfortunately, I have to get home now and cannot wait anymore for her. Perhaps she has already left the castle on her own."

At that moment the shuttle bus arrived. If Héctor had had any sense, he would not have climbed onto the bus with his sister, who, it was obvious, had found out where he was living and had come to find Arietta. But Héctor wasn't thinking straight. The fight with Arietta had upset him very much. He had only wanted her to stay one more night, and she had refused, and then he'd had to lock her cloak up in a chest (this time he really did lock it, whereas the day before he only *said* he'd locked it), and she had gotten so very mad at him, he'd had to lock her away, too.

The shuttle bus was so crowded, Héctor did not have to sit next to Silvia, but once they were on the Number 6 bus heading downtown, there were some empty seats. Silvia clearly expected the old lady to sit next to her.

"So," Silvia said when they were finally settled, "were you able to speak to the pigeons and find out anything? Why they're so big and everything?"

Héctor frowned. "They don't know anything," he said, guessing at an answer and trying at the same time to sound creaky.

"Oh my, you sound as if you've caught a cold," said Silvia. "This journey might have been too much for you. Here, please"—she scrabbled in her bag and brought out a packet of horrid-looking brown powder—"try some of these dried kiwi skins. They will make you feel better."

"Oh no, no, I'll be fine," said Héctor. If that wasn't just like Silvia—dried kiwi skins! How disgusting!

"The pigeons knew nothing at all?" Silvia persisted.

Héctor shook his head and coughed slightly. "I am so weary. I think I shall close my eyes."

"Yes, yes, of course. I'll wake you up presently," said Silvia.

While Héctor closed his eyes and pretended to snooze Silvia glanced at him from time to time. It began to dawn on her that the old lady had been wearing a different coat from the one she was wearing now. And gloves? She hadn't been wearing gloves. And the old lady certainly hadn't taken up so much of the seat before. Silvia felt positively squeezed against the window.

No, something definitely was different—this was the old lady's face, but not her legs. No one on earth had long, skinny legs like these except for . . . and then she realized, of course, that once again her brother was using someone else's face.

Ooh, she wanted to pinch him! She wanted to *poke* him, pull his old-lady nose, even bite his arm. That would show him!

But she contained herself. She stared out the window and tried to think. First of all, what had happened to the poor old lady?

How had Héctor managed to get her face? He must have harmed her in some way! And now here he was, sitting right next to her, not knowing she knew who he was. Perhaps she could use this knowledge to her advantage.

What Silvia did not realize was that Ula, Pitter, and Patter had been looking out the tower window and had seen Silvia get on the bus. "My friends," Ula had said, turning to the birds, "you must fly down and follow that bus. And when that lady gets off, you must approach her, and no matter where she goes, you must not leave her side. I hope that gradually she will understand that I have sent you. You must somehow let her know that Arietta is being kept here against her will. *Against her will*—do you understand that? And please also let her know that I am all right. I don't want her worrying about me on top of everything else."

Ula was lucky that Pitter and Patter were her choice of messengers. The two birds were happy to embark on this mission. The evening before, they had discovered they liked Sam and Belle's chocolate more than the master's chocolate (Sam and Belle had rewarded them with two chocolate cupcakes).

And so as Silvia was trying to figure out what to do about Héctor, she began to notice that at every bus stop (and there were many— the bus was a local, so it stopped frequently) there were two oversized pigeons just hanging about. What was this? Had Héctor brought them along as bodyguards? She shuddered slightly, but then peering at them intently, she was quite sure they were the same two pigeons who had come to the deli last night. By the end of the evening, those pigeons had not seemed frightening at all.

17

Silvia began to feel the dawning of hope. Could it be? Could it be these pigeons were coming with further word of Arietta? With word of the old lady?

Héctor groaned and stirred slightly. He hated sitting next to his sister. He didn't think he could last much longer. Silvia jabbed him sharply with her elbow. "Oh, dear me, excuse me," she said, pretending to be sorry, "but it is a tight squeeze in here. I hope you have had a nice little nap, but now that you are awake, I was wondering if you would be willing to teach me some Pigeonish."

Héctor gave a fake yawn and rubbed his face. What in the world was she talking about?

"I think your life is so fascinating," said Silvia. "I'd love you to come home to my apartment. I'll make a nice dinner, and you can teach me some of the bird dialects."

But Héctor had had enough. "I really must get out at the next stop," he said. Before Silvia could do or say anything, Héctor jumped up and pushed and jostled his way off the bus.

"Old ladies ain't what they used to be," the bus driver remarked.

Silvia was torn between following Héctor and going back to the Mink Street Deli to see if Arietta was home yet. Before she could decide, the bus had already moved on, so she stayed on it, all the way to 21st Street.

And there the giant pigeons were when she got off.

While Silvia had been at the bus stop waiting for Arietta she had snipped the needles off a little evergreen bush she had been sitting next to. She always carried a small pair of scissors with her for that purpose. Her grandfather, her darling *abuelito,* had taught her to do that a long time ago, when he had still lived with the family. Silvia sighed. Oh, Abuelito! There was hardly a day that Silvia didn't think of him for one reason or another. He was the one who had gotten her started on food magic.

Now, this evergreen by the bus stop was a sort of mint, and it was so aromatic, she had nibbled a bit of it. The herb had many different names—Silvia knew it as Thirst-Tea because you could chew it when your mouth was dry, and it was as refreshing as drinking a large glass of water. What Silvia didn't realize was that in some parts of the world, the plant is called Bird-Speak because it enables you, just for a short time, to speak with the first bird you meet after you ingest it.

So as Pitter and Patter approached Silvia she was, to her amazement, able to understand their chatter.

"I hope we get some of Sam and Belle's chocolate again," Pitter was saying.

"Yeah, that was yummy," Patter said.

Silvia stood listening for a moment, just enjoying the sensation of understanding their speech. Then it occurred to her that if she could understand them, maybe they could understand her. She leaned down and said, "Hello, how are you?"

Pitter and Patter nearly bobbled over backward. "Can *you* speak Pigeonish, too?" they asked in astonishment.

"I seem to be able to, just for the moment, anyway," she said. "Did you see an old lady at the castle by any chance?"

"Yes," said Pitter. "She wanted you to know she is all right. She is with the girl called Arietta."

"¡Qué bueno!" Silvia gasped, holding a hand up to her heart. "And Arietta, how is she?"

Pitter looked at Patter, and Patter looked at Pitter. "Well, we don't think she likes being locked in the tower room," Pitter finally said. "But she is all right besides that."

"Locked in a room," Silvia fumed. "Now listen to me. You must come and tell Sam and Belle everything you know."

Pitter and Patter exchanged a delighted glance—more of Sam and Belle's chocolate!— and waddled happily with Silvia down the several blocks to 21st Street. Silvia marched briskly into the deli, the birds following.

"Oh, Silvia, where is Arietta?" Sam and Belle rushed toward her. "Weren't you able to find her?"

"I'm afraid my brother is keeping her at the Castle," said Silvia.

"Keeping her! What do you mean?" Sam and Belle looked at Silvia, horrified.

Silvia quickly gestured toward the birds. "You remember Pitter and Patter. Well, I've discovered I can speak their language, so they can tell us what has happened."

The pigeons bowed politely. "We are delighted to see you again," said Pitter.

"We're so sorry about everything," said Patter.

Silvia translated what to Sam and Belle sounded like cooing and billing.

"Ask them why Héctor is keeping her," Belle said, wringing her hands.

Silvia related the question in Pigeonish, but as they began to answer, the power of the Bird-Speak had worn off. "Wait, wait," she cried. By now she realized why she had been able to speak to the birds. Luckily, she had collected quite a bit of the plant. She pulled out a sprig and nibbled, and thank goodness, the cooing suddenly bubbled into words.

"Success!" cried Silvia. She quickly handed Sam and Belle some of the Bird-Speak. "Here, just eat a little of this and then the pigeons will be able to tell you all about Arietta themselves."

"Perhaps before we go on, we could have just a little of that chocolate cake?" Pitter asked shyly, looking longingly into the glass case where all the goodies were.

Belle quickly realized it made more sense to brew a whole pot of Bird-Speak. Sam brought out the chocolate cake. As they sat around one of the little round tables at the deli Pitter and Patter related every little detail about Arietta that Sam and Belle could think to ask.

18

Héctor returned home to the Castle in a very grumpy mood. It had been a terrible idea to go out into the world with an old lady's face. People did not treat him well at all. They either completely ignored him or were impatient, or condescending, or rude. And this was so surprising to Héctor. Couldn't they see how beautiful Ula's face was? And weren't people supposed to be nice to old ladies?

Weary and discouraged, Héctor climbed the stairs to the Castle tower carrying a bag of artichokes. It would cheer him up, at least, to see Arietta. And then he would make her a nice dinner, and then maybe they could play another game of hide-and-seek.

Imagine his surprise when he walked into the tower room and found the old lady whose face he had worn all afternoon! She was sitting in a heavy fourteenth-century chair. Arietta was fast asleep in the canopy bed.

Héctor was now wearing his own face, so at least Ula didn't have to be shocked at the sight of her own face. But nevertheless, she *was* shocked because this man looked just like her own dear departed husband, Oscar.

"My grandson. *¡Mi gatito precioso, mi pollito!* My precious little kitten, my little chicken!" Ula threw herself out of the chair and stood with her arms open wide.

Héctor didn't seem to be able to take in

what she was saying. "Who are you? How did you get here? What are you doing here?"

"You should know very well who I am, and I flew up here, and I'm looking after Arietta," said Ula calmly. "Please don't raise your voice; you'll wake her up. I've been singing songs in Nightingalish all afternoon to make her feel better about being locked up here, and she finally fell asleep. Now, *mi amor,* come sit beside me. I'd like to hear all about you, why you're living in this castle, and why you're keeping this poor child."

Héctor stood rooted to the floor, his eyes wide and staring. "Who are you?" he asked again.

"*Héctor, soy tu abuela, ¿no me recuerdas?* Is it possible you don't remember me? I am your very own *abuelita!*"

"Abuelita!" Héctor fell to his knees. He couldn't believe it. Here was his very own *abuelita!* Oh, no wonder he had instantly and instinctively adored that face! "Abuelita," he said again, hoarsely. "Why didn't you say something before, when you saw me?"

"When did I see you, *mi amor?*"

Héctor realized he hadn't been wearing his own face when she approached him asking for directions. He shivered slightly. How terrible! They had almost missed each other because he had not looked like himself!

"But why—why did you come here? Did you know I was here?"

"No, I did not know," said Ula. "I came here to speak to the pigeons. And then I was asked to look for a girl named Arietta."

"Who asked you?" Héctor demanded, but even as he asked, he knew the answer.

"Why, a very nice woman I sat with on the bus. She seemed afraid of running into you, so she asked me to find Arietta. When did you become such a frightening person, Héctor? You used to be such a nice little boy!"

Héctor groaned. "That was Silvia you sat next to," he said.

"Silvia!" Ula was overcome. What a terrible thing! She had not recognized her own grandchild, and her own grandchild had not recognized her. That's what came of being separated for almost thirty years. It was almost more than she could bear.

But now she had the safety of the little girl to think about. "Really, Héctor, what are you thinking? Why would you keep a child here against her will?"

Even though Ula and Héctor had not seen each other for as long as thirty years, it seemed perfectly natural for Ula to be scolding Héctor. She always had been a bit of a scold, but such a loving scold!

"It wasn't against her will," said Héctor. "She came here all by herself."

"But you're not letting her go," said Ula sternly.

Héctor sighed deeply. He looked at the sleeping Arietta. When he looked at this girl, in the deepest place of his heart he knew he was not ugly.

As Ula looked at Arietta she too felt unusually peaceful. She had traveled the globe interviewing birds, believing they had answers to the mysteries of life, hoping, perhaps, to fill the loneliness of losing first her daughter (because she married a man who did not want her to practice magic), and then her grandchildren, and then her husband. Looking down at Arietta, Ula no longer felt the urge to travel. This child captivated her heart. And best of all, she had brought her back to Héctor.

"Now you must let her go home, Héctor," she said.

But surprisingly, Héctor said, "No. I have

decided that I must not let her go. She is the one person in all my life who never made me feel ugly. If anyone comes to take her away, I will send out my soon-to-be-formed Pigeon Army. And even you, Abuelita, cannot stop me."

19

Ruth named herself General of the Pigeon Army. Every day on the upper courtyard, she put the pigeons through drills, marching them in orderly lines, practicing lunging and diving, advancing with beaks wide open. Every day the maneuvers were gaining in precision and viciousness.

And soon they were put into practice. For Sam and Belle called the police again, and this time they knew where to go. But as the cops got out of their squad cars and approached the Castle the pigeons dove down and attacked. In a matter of moments three men had to be taken off to the emergency room.

While the police were regrouping and figuring out what to do next—rumor had it they were calling in the National Guard—word of the newly formed army traveled to Pitter and Patter through pigeon prattle. How fortunate those two pigeons felt they were to have left the Castle. The thought of marching around to Ruth's orders made their wings ache. She had always been a bossy one.

Pitter and Patter also learned about Ula and related the news to Silvia.

"Mi abuelita," she kept saying over and over again. She could not get over the fact she had sat next to her own grandmother on the bus and hadn't even recognized her. But then, the truth was, she had been so little when

Abuelita had left. She had never understood it—one day Ula was filling the whole house with her presence, with her brisk energy, her lively eyes, her knowledge of food magic, her bright birds, her loving heart, and the next, she was gone.

How sad she and Héctor had been the day their grandparents had left the house. Come to think of it, it was on that very day they had started to fight with each other, and then the fighting had never stopped. Oh, how tiring and annoying to fight with your brother all the time!

And now—just think of it—Abuelita was living with Héctor only one hundred blocks to the north, as his captive, no less, as he was keeping her locked up along with Arietta.

The police were having a harder time rescuing Arietta than anyone could believe.

For one thing, a group of animal lovers had surrounded the Castle, intending to make sure no violence was used against the pigeons. Giant or not, they deserved to be protected. Someone had suggested a helicopter come in and swoop by the tower window, but no one could be found who would attempt this risky maneuver. So for the moment, things were at a standstill.

Sam and Belle, Silvia, Pitter and Patter, and Gus (who had raced over to the deli as soon as he understood that Arietta had been kidnapped) decided they needed to take Arietta's rescue into their own hands.

"*Bueno,*" Silvia said, standing before the others who sat at a table in the deli. "I am sure if we put our heads together, we can come up with a plan."

"We could stir up a rebel army of pigeons," said Patter. "Counter-pigeon strike."

"It would be small pigeons against the hefty pigeons," Pitter said doubtfully. "The master seems to be the only one who can feed chocolate to us and make us grow larger. Even though," he said with a small nod in Sam and Belle's direction, "your chocolate is far superior."

Patter sighed. "You're right. The big pigeons would demolish the small pigeons." She shuddered slightly at the thought, for both she and Pitter, without the benefit of Héctor's magic, were slowly returning to their former size.

Gus was looking out the window. Now, suddenly, he stood up, causing the chair he had been sitting on to fall over backward.

"Cats!" he cried out. "The answer is cats!" Everyone followed his glance. He was looking at Xiaolu, who was sitting in the window of the Smiling Dragon Restaurant.

Belle's usually rosy cheeks were pale, her eyes swollen with weeping; but now, at the thought of a solution, new color crept back into her face.

"It's an idea," said Sam, looking thoughtfully over at Xiaolu.

Pitter and Patter looked unenthusiastic. There had been plenty of cats in their old neighborhood. Always creeping up on one when one least expected it. Nasty critters!

"But my Cattish is limited," Gus said. "I was two when I left the cats, and I might not have a large enough vocabulary to tell them what needs to be done."

Everyone looked at one another. How would they be able to communicate their plight to the cats?

"Ivan's bookstore is down the street," said Sam, who was not going to be discouraged. "He might have a Cattish dictionary."

Sam, Gus, and Silvia immediately set out from the deli and went down the street to Ivan's secondhand bookstore. Belle stayed behind with the pigeons in case there were customers.

When Sam stepped into the bookstore and found Ivan at the front desk, he immediately came right to the point. "We're going to try to rescue Arietta, and to do so, we need a dictionary in Cattish."

"English-to-Cattish or Cattish-to-English?" Ivan asked.

"Both," said Silvia.

Ivan got up from behind his desk, which was a sign of how upset he was by the situation. Usually he stayed behind the desk and pointed to the aisle where people might or might not be able to find the books they were looking for. But Ivan loved Arietta and wanted to be as helpful as possible.

He went straight to the back of the store and climbed up a ladder on wheels, which was attached to the bookcase. From the twelfth shelf he pulled out the sixth book from the left. He blew the dust off it and climbed down and handed the book to Sam.

"I was sure it was still here," said Ivan. "Not many people come in looking for a Cattish dictionary these days. There was a sort of fad for Cattish during one of the plagues. Everyone wanted to learn it because they wanted the cats to get rid of the rats, but that was, of course, a long time ago."

Sam held the old book in his hands. The cover was green, now faded to gray green. In gold letters it read: *A Compendium of the Cattish Tongue with Translation to English and also the English Tongue with Translation to Cattish.*

It fell open to a list of Commonly Used Expressions:

"Cat got your tongue?"

"Curiosity killed the cat." (Considered impolite)

"A cat has nine lives." (A compliment)

"This is just what we need," said Sam. "Thank you so much, Ivan, and please come over soon for a cup of coffee."

"Sure, sure, and you'll have Arietta back in no time," said Ivan. He ran his fingers through his thick silvery hair. "And the book's on me—no charge."

20

Silvia sat with Gus in a sunny corner of the Mink Street Deli, and together they pored over the dictionary. Silvia had always been able to learn languages easily, a skill she had probably inherited from Ula, and now she found Cattish had elements of both Gaelic and Chinese in it. Gus found it easy to build on what he already knew.

Soon Gus ventured across the street to the Smiling Dragon. He asked Xiaolu to come back to the deli. Pitter and Patter, shrinking back to their old size, were too nervous to sit around the table with her, and decided to retire to the back room.

Belle offered Xiaolu a dish of salmon, and then she and Sam also went to the back room and waited, thinking that Silvia and Gus would be able to concentrate better if they weren't around.

Xiaolu was delighted with the salmon. When she had finished eating, she sat on the table delicately cleaning her whiskers with a white paw. Silvia began speaking to her in halting Cattish.

Cattish has several thousand dialects, and Silvia was afraid Xiaolu wouldn't understand her accent; but the cat's ears perked right up, and she stopped washing in mid-lick.

"How extraordinary," the cat exclaimed. "You seem to have picked up my language very quickly."

"Sorry, I no very good," Silvia said apologetically.

"No, no," Xiaolu said enthusiastically. "Very very good!"

Silvia and Gus went on to lay out the whole problem. It took a while because they kept having to look up words in the dictionary, and some of the words sounded so much like other words, there were misunderstandings.

For instance, the Cattish word for "pigeons" is *mi-ach,* but Silvia pronounced it *mi-eouch,* which means "frogs." Xiaolu thought she was wanted to fight a battle against giant frogs. And then, certain words don't exist in Cattish, like *chocolate.* So Silvia had a hard time explaining how Héctor had been able to make the pigeons grow. Gus hit on calling it magic food because, not surprisingly, there were several words for magic in Cattish.

Gus also realized that it was important to make it clear that the cats would be rewarded handsomely. Anytime they were hungry, he told Xiaolu, Sam and Belle's door would be open to them.

Once Xiaolu had a good grasp of the situation, she twitched her ears and said, "The offer of free, delectable food, that is incentive for any cat," she said, "but we shall do this because Arietta is a child, and children should not be taken from their mothers and fathers. But," she added, putting her ears back, "we must approach the problem not just with force but with cunning."

She leaped off the table and began pacing back and forth across the floor of the deli.

Silvia and Gus waited.

Flick, flick, Xiaolu's tail sliced the air like a dangerous sword. Finally she leaped back up onto the table.

"I have in mind an ancient tale," she said. "A tale, meaning a story, not the prolongation of my rear end." She flicked her tail expressively and laughed a dry laugh. (*Tail* and *tale* in Cattish, as in English, actually do sound the same but are spelled differently.) "There is a story that has been passed down through the centuries—of how after many years of war, one army constructed a giant cat out of wood and wheeled it just outside the gates of the enemy's city. The gates, being made of stone, had always been too slippery for the cats of the attacking army to scale. The citizens within the city thought the wooden cat was an offering from the gods and pulled it inside. Little did they know the cat was hollow, and filled with enemy soldiers."

Silvia did not catch every word Xiaolu spoke, but she understood the gist of it. "I always thought it was a giant horse, not a cat," she said.

Xiaolu twitched her ears indignantly. "A horse! That's ridiculous! What a silly idea! But in any case, I believe we must construct a giant pigeon and bring it to the castle."

"It will be hollow!" Gus yelled, catching on to the idea.

"And filled with cats!" Silvia finished happily.

She scooped up Xiaolu and began dancing with her around the room. "*¡Qué maravilloso plan! ¡Qué plan supremo!* The cat is a genius!"

Xiaolu sprang out of her arms and sat under a chair.

"Cats only dance with other cats," Gus explained.

"I believe we are finished for the moment," Xiaolu said stiffly. "I will gather a militia of the strongest, fiercest cats in the city. I will train them. You may trust me to do my part. But you humans must build the pigeon. When you are ready, I shall be ready. You know where to find me."

With that Xiaolu whisked her way over to the door, stretched up on her hind legs, allowed her full weight to fall on the door handle, and pulled. With her head held high she made a grand exit.

Pitter, Patter, and Sam returned from the back room, and Belle brewed up a pot of Bird-Speak. (Silvia had discovered a health food store where she could buy it in the actual form of tea.) And then the six of them sat until it was well past midnight discussing the plan and possible problems.

Sam was worried there might be a legend in pigeon lore that told of a similar trick. But Pitter and Patter both said no, they had never heard such a story.

"Who can we get to build the pigeon?" Silvia asked.

Sam and Belle looked at each other.

"Mr. Mann!" they shouted at the same time.

2-1

The very next day as soon as the shops along Mink Street opened, Sam and Belle walked down the street to the store where Mr. Mann made and sold grandfather clocks and music boxes.

Walking into Mr. Mann's store was like walking into an enchanted world. Music boxes were playing, grandfather clocks were ticking, or chiming, or cuckooing, depending on when you arrived. In some of the boxes and clocks you could see the inner workings, intricate cogs and wheels, little pieces of metal that plinked out different tunes—only Mr. Mann's music boxes didn't plink. They made lovely bell-like sounds that made you want to stop whatever you were doing and listen. It was well-known that Mr. Mann had won his wife by giving her music boxes. The one that finally melted her heart played a song called "Spotted Neckties in July." It was a song only the hardest-hearted person could resist.

Mr. Mann was thrilled to be asked to help rescue Arietta. It had hurt him dreadfully to think someone had taken Sam and Belle's lovely child. His mind was instantly filled with ideas for the giant, hollow pigeon. He would make the eyes blink, the wings flutter. As busy as he was, and he *was* busy—people from all over the world ordered clocks and music boxes from him—he would make a spectacular giant pigeon before the week was over.

Mr. Mann went to work. His first task was to design the pigeon. He sat at his desk and made drawing after drawing until he was satisfied.

The next task was to go to his warehouse to select the wood. He chose boards from many different kinds of trees—hop hornbeam and hickory, oak and maple, birch and black locust, and white ash. It was all dried and seasoned and cured so none of it would crack or warp or shrink, very important considerations when you are making anything from wood.

Finally, he began steaming the boards so they would bend into lovely pigeon curves. Each day he spent hours planing, sanding, gluing, clamping. He worked feverishly for four days, eating and sleeping in his workshop so that he could make the best use of his time.

During that week Xiaolu had also been busy. Word traveled quickly throughout the cat community. A human child had been kidnapped by pigeons. *Pigeons!* Some of the cats had trouble swallowing the story, believing that some bellicose tomcat was spreading the story just to cause trouble. The calico cats didn't like fighting at all and flatly refused to believe a word of it, until Xiaolu asked Silvia to speak directly to one of the calico leaders.

From Silvia the calicos learned that pigeons hadn't really stolen Arietta. It had been a man. So the calicos agreed that this one time only would they join the battle.

The orange cats, of course, were fiercely loyal to Gus, and by association, Arietta; they signed up almost at once.

Frithby, a gray squirrel who had overheard this conversation, thought a fight against giant pigeons might be a battle worth fighting. Frithby had seen some of those giant pigeons strutting around. They made the fur on his back stand up. Appointing himself Ambassador of the Squirrels, he went to speak to Xiaolu and asked if the squirrels could join the battle.

"I do recognize," said Xiaolu, "that the squirrels might be helpful, but it is difficult to imagine how the cats and squirrels will get along with each other, stuffed together, as they will be, in the cramped and dark interior of the wooden pigeon."

"Perhaps," said Frithby, "the cats can stay in the bow of the pigeon, while the squirrels can be confined to the midships and the stern." Because Frithby lived by the pond in the park, he had picked up a lot of nautical lore from the people who sailed miniature sailboats there.

22

As dawn was breaking on the fifth day, Ula awoke with a start. She couldn't sleep anymore. She was stabbed through and through with worry. Héctor was talking more and more about *adopting* Arietta. *Adopting* her! How could he even consider such a thing? When had her Héctor become so crazy? Oh, why had she and Oscar stayed away so long? Because their feelings had been hurt, their pride had been hurt. Oh, silly pride!

Besides being upset with Héctor, Ula was also finding the pigeons increasingly annoying. They were such incessant gossips! All day long she heard things like, "Can you believe Uncle Harry moved from the East Side to the West Side? He has no business moving at his age." Ula longed for a conversation with another kind of bird—even crows would be refreshing, or blue jays.

Ula made up her mind to avoid the pigeons altogether by spending the day in the gardens. Héctor allowed Ula (but never Arietta, who, he was sure, would get away from him if he once allowed her out of the tower) to ramble there. Ruth kept lookouts posted so she couldn't escape.

Ula decided the time to head out was right now. The birds were active early in the morning. It would be the best time for good conversation. She walked down the stairs and out a back door, which, of course, was much easier to open than the massive front door with its scary portcullis, through which the public entered every day.

As she made her way she wondered what had happened to Pitter and Patter. Had they not been able to keep up with Silvia's bus? She would speak to a group of sparrows she often saw twittering about and send them to find Silvia. She wished she had thought to do this sooner.

Héctor, meanwhile, was preparing himself to go meet with a lawyer about adopting Arietta. He was ready with a good story—how she'd been abandoned on his doorstep, how he'd taken her in and raised her.

He nibbled a few peanuts to make himself smaller and then, sticking his head out the window, whistled for a pigeon to take him into town. At the last minute he put on the face he'd been saving just for this purpose. He'd discovered he could keep faces longer than six hours if he kept the magic looking glass in the freezer overnight. Now he took it out, letting it warm up a bit before he put the face on. It was the face of a middle-aged woman with round, plump cheeks and kind eyes. Just right, he thought, for softening up the lawyer. It felt a little cold, and as yet it was hard to smile, but by the time he reached the lawyer's, he knew it would be warmed up and ready to charm. From his growing collection of outfits, he selected a pink sweater and a pair of tan slacks.

On the dawn of the fifth morning, at the same time that Ula and Héctor were engaged in their respective activities, an army of cats and squirrels assembled in the park in front of a statue of a general riding a horse. Xiaolu and Frithby were perched on either shoulder of the general, ready to shout orders.

Silvia and Gus stood on the ground, just in front. Silvia had instructed Sam and Belle to stay at the deli, and under no circumstances were they to leave. They must be home at the deli when Arietta returned.

A cheer rose up as Mr. Mann, sitting directly behind the left eye, drove a giant wooden pigeon on wheels into the park. It was a marvelous sight to behold. Mr. Mann had painted it gray, but it was delicately tinted with phosphorescent greens and blues, and of course, there was a gleaming white ring around its neck.

Pressing a button, Mr. Mann made the wings flap, the beady eyes blink.

Once more, a great cheer rose up.

The cheering of the cats and squirrels made shivers run through the humans. Gus, who had joined the throng, soon found himself pushed along by the flow of hundreds of animals as they began to stream up the gang-plank into the hollow interior of the pigeon.

"Squirrels to the stern, cats to the bow," a large tabby cat kept intoning at the entrance to the pigeon.

Gus, of course, joined the cats, and went with them to the bow of the pigeon.

Silvia climbed into the cockpit with Mr. Mann. The eyes of the pigeon were the windows to the outside world. Mr. Mann pressed a button, and slowly the gangplank swung up, and then with a click, shut tight, blending seamlessly into the side.

All light within the pigeon was extinguished. Fortunately, Mr. Mann had drilled ventilation holes every three feet or so, so there was enough air coming in; however, the atmosphere quickly became pungent. Luckily for him, Gus rather liked the smell.

The animals had been instructed to be

deathly still and silent, and so they were, except for the occasional need to scratch. They were quiet even as Mr. Mann pressed a button, and with a click and a whir the wooden wings of the pigeon began to flap, and miraculously, the whole creation lifted up off the ground.

It was very early in the morning—light was only just creeping into the sky. Few people were up and about, but those who were—did they look up and see a monstrosity of a pigeon winging its way over their heads? And if they did, what did they think?

It was a city where anything could happen, and often did, and so perhaps what the people saw did not amaze them for long.

23

Silvia, for her part, *was* amazed, and kept on being so—to be flying above the trees, the streets, the buildings, in a pigeon-shaped ship filled with cats and squirrels! Never in her wildest dreams had she imagined she would be doing such a thing. Her heart thumped happily as she thought that soon they would be freeing her darling Arietta from the clutches of her dastardly brother. There, rapidly coming closer, were the towers of the

Castle. Oh, Arietta, she thought to herself, we're coming!

There was a slight lurching as Mr. Mann began the descent to the parking lot, the place where the big tour buses usually pulled up. All around him Gus heard a rustling as the animals sat up and stretched as best they could in cramped quarters.

Ruth was the first pigeon to notice the strange apparition. She was sitting on the ledge of the window of the tower room, keeping one beady eye out for Ula while the other eye roamed the upper courtyard.

There had been some unrest among the pigeons lately. It seemed as if some of them were homesick for their old neighborhoods. The pigeons didn't much like military life. It was exhausting and not much fun.

Ruth was not happy about these hints of rebellion. She was enjoying her life at the

Castle. Since first flying there, she'd found herself in a position of authority. She'd discovered she had a real knack for bossing other pigeons around.

As she looked down at the pigeons in the courtyard she was watching to see if any of them were banding together, plotting against her. And that is when her eye was caught by the spectacle of the giant pigeon landing in the parking lot of the Castle.

At first, Ruth felt a sort of terror. She shielded her eyes with a wing. But then, slowly, slowly, she peeked around and looked. This time the sight was less terrifying and more awe-inspiring. It was a pigeon, after all, a familiar shape, something not to be frightened of, but to be revered.

From the sudden commotion in the courtyard, it was apparent the others had now noticed the great bird. Ruth fluttered down to join them.

"What is it? What is it? What is it?" The pigeons rushed toward Ruth, their heads bobbing in consternation.

"It's a goddess!" pronounced Ruth, who was pretty sure it was, but not absolutely sure; but the moment the words were out of her beak, it sounded like the truth.

"A goddess, goddess, goddess," the pigeons cooed in wonder.

The pigeons rose up as one from the courtyard. Moving more like a swarm of bees than a flock of birds, they zoomed straight down and landed on the lawn several yards away from the pigeon.

Spying the giant bird from above was nothing to how it now appeared to them. It was enormous! They were dwarfed by the majesty of its bulk! And now, as they gazed in rapt wonder, the wings of the goddess swept up, and her eyes blinked.

A coo of awe and fear rose up from the pigeons. They fell forward on their beaks, covering their heads with their wings.

"O mighty goddess," Ruth began.

"Mighty goddess, mighty goddess, mighty goddess," the pigeons echoed.

There was a slight whirring, and then a click. The pigeons, whose eyes were clamped shut, thought the goddess was speaking to them. They did not see the ramp swing down. They did not see Xiaolu and Frithby advancing with scores of fiercely scowling cats and squirrels. They did not see a hundred bodies poised to lunge and bite and claw and scratch.

But before the first bloodthirsty battle cry could escape from the throats of the attackers, in his excitement Mr. Mann inadvertently pressed another button. More of an artist than a warrior, Mr. Mann had built a music box just behind the pigeon's beak, and now, beautiful bell-like chimes filled the air.

Poised to strike, the animals halted in mid-gesture. Cats, squirrels, and the boy, Gus, who had also come down the ramp, all fell into a dreaming sleep.

24

The cats dreamed of sunlit window seats filled with plump cushions. The squirrels dreamed of bird feeders that human beings never forgot to fill. Gus dreamed he was dancing with the cats. The pigeons dreamed of their homes, each one seeing his or her particular ledge or sidewalk.

Mr. Mann, too, sat at his steering wheel high up in the cockpit and dreamed he was dancing with Mrs. Mann; Silvia, who was just coming down the stairs from the beak, sat on the top step and dreamed of Héctor and Ula and Oscar, of Pepe and María. They had come to visit, and she was serving them squash soup, which if you eat under a full moon will stop you from fighting with your relatives.

Arietta, way up in the tower room, slept in the canopy bed. She dreamed of freshly baked bread and hot pastrami sandwiches. She felt her mother's strong arms around her and heard her father's deep laugh.

And in the gardens, where she had walked all morning conversing with sparrows, crows, and blue jays, Ula also dreamed. She was in the middle of a flock of birds with rainbow-colored feathers; the head bird was Oscar, and he was leading her home to live with her family.

The old stones that made up the Castle dreamed of glaciers and dinosaurs, and inside, even the wood that formed the old chests and chairs and tables—yes, the old, old wood—dreamed of the forests they had come from, where boars roamed, and unicorns, and the lock on one of the old chests sprang open, and the lid flew up.

The tip of a green leaf poked out, and then another and another. The music had awakened the cloak, and now it was eager to find its owner.

Héctor was flying home.

He was elated. The interview had gone well. In a few days the adoption papers would arrive.

Spotting the large form of the wooden pigeon from a distance, Héctor thought a tourist bus had arrived early, and in his happy mood he forgot that tourists had not been allowed to visit the Castle because of the attacking pigeons. He decided to fly down and greet the tourists, let them in before opening time today. His eyes, in any case, quickly flicked away from the pigeon and over to the tower window.

"Oh, Arietta, *hija de mi corazón,* daughter of my heart," he was murmuring under his breath as his pigeon began her descent. He didn't see the tableau spread out beneath him: the great wooden pigeon, the overgrown live pigeons with their heads bent and their eyes closed, the cats and squirrels baring their teeth, young Gus crouching in the middle of them. Every creature was frozen as if posing for one of those huge paintings of battles you see in museums.

Just as Héctor's pigeon touched down, the music ended. Hundreds of pairs of eyes blinked, heads shook, mouths shut with a snap before they opened again in order to roar fiercely. And now the battle began in earnest.

Héctor stood paralyzed, watching in horror as cats and squirrels advanced and slashed

viciously at the pigeons. Ruth's training had paid off—a few pigeons instinctively attacked back, using beaks and claws. Feathers and fur flew up above the fray. The sound of screams and squawking rent the air.

Ruth had been close to one of the wheels of the wooden pigeon when she had fallen asleep, so now she was partially obscured from the attackers. She was able to stand and observe: she saw the ramp and the open door, and realized with a shock it was all a trick. Gathering her wits, she flew up and perched on the top of the wheel and began to shout orders.

"Fly up," she screamed above the din. "Fly up! Use your wings! You can fly, and they can't!"

A few pigeons heard her, and those that did not have damaged wings flew up and began to attack from the air. Blood trickled from the exposed faces of the cats and squirrels; soon, however, the cats ran up the ramp and sprang with mighty leaps into the air, sharp claws extended. The squirrels scaled the trunks of several birch trees that grew right by the parking lot, and then flung themselves from the topmost branches onto the pigeons.

Silvia watched it all in horror. How was this to end? How would Arietta ever be rescued in this way? And then she saw—streaming out of one of the tower windows—Arietta. She was cloaked in artichoke leaves, with only her face visible.

One by one the heads of the animals tilted up. As they watched, the animals forgot to fight. They collapsed in heaps upon the ground—squirrels, cats, pigeons, all mixed up together, whimpering or silent, licking their wounds.

As for Héctor . . . Héctor stood, his arms raised to the air, tears running down his face. "Arie! Arie!" he cried. "Arietta, don't leave me!" He had one last glimpse of her before the cloak, curling about her, lifted her up higher and higher, and then, straightening, shot away, faster and faster until she was as small as a bird, and then only a speck retreating into the haze that hung over the city.

Héctor fell to the ground, and as he did so, the magic looking glass, which was tucked inside his pocket, smashed into little pieces.

25

Silvia began to move about the wounded, applying the salves she carried in her pouch. Xiaolu, knowledgeable in ancient Chinese healing techniques, stayed by her side and helped.

A great many pigeons were bleeding profusely. A few cats suffered from bad pecks. Some of the squirrels could only see out of one eye, and Frithby, who had been very brave in the meleé, had a very sore tail. It was a good thing the battle had lasted only a short time, or there would have been many more wounded.

Mr. Mann emerged from the pigeon. "Where's the boy?" he asked, looking around. "Gus? What's happened to him?"

"Gus!" Silvia exclaimed. She had completely forgotten about him.

And then they found him. He was lying in a heap on the ground, surrounded by a half a dozen orange cats. Uncle was licking a cut over the boy's right eye; the other cats were attending his arms and hands, which were terribly slashed and bleeding.

"He was trying to defend me," said Uncle, looking up when he saw Silvia. Silvia was glad she had learned enough Cattish so she could understand him. "They attacked him good and forced him off the ramp, but not before he got *them* good, with his bare hands!"

Groaning, Gus tried to sit up. "One of 'em

picked Uncle up and was about to carry him away, so I reached up and grabbed him, and that's when two pigeons came at me, one in the front, one from behind."

"He's a brave lad, is our Gus—one of our own," Uncle said proudly. "Lie back down, boy, and we'll take care of you."

And now, in spite of herself, Silvia found herself walking toward Héctor. His true face was showing through in the places where his tears had run. She paused for a moment, looking at him. She felt her heart softening a bit. It wasn't such a bad face. Why, she wondered, had she blamed him all these years for Abuelita and Abuelito leaving? She thought with longing of those days when the two of them still played and got along, and the dream came back to her: squash soup and family, all under a full moon.

Maybe, she thought, maybe if she could find just the right squash—acorn, or butternut . . . or maybe zucchini? Yes, she would figure out which one, and then—her heart squeezed a bit—the dream might come true. She walked over to Héctor and put a hand on his shoulder.

"*Cálmate, mi hermanito,*" she said, sitting down beside him. "You still have me, your sister. Whether you like it or not, I am not going to fly away from you."

Ula, by this time, had come up the path from the gardens. She surveyed the scene before her with dismay. Pigeons, cats, and squirrels were lying everywhere. Oh, what an extraordinary morning it had been! First, just as she had been having a good laugh with a blue jay, there had been the appearance of that giant pigeon—so frightening and unexpected. But before she could wonder at it too much, she'd fallen into a dream—such a lovely dream, of flying with Oscar, flying home to family. But then terrible screams and battle cries had wrenched her from the dream. She had not dared take one step until she'd looked up and had seen Arietta flying away from the Castle, wearing the artichoke cloak she had spoken of so often during the days and nights the two of them had spent together. Ah, Arietta, that dear child! She had escaped and was flying home, she could only hope, to her mother and father! Her heart felt lighter than it had in days.

But Héctor, Ula knew, would be crushed. As angry as she had been at him, all her anger melted now she knew that Arietta was free. She had better see what she could do for him.

As she approached Héctor, Ula thought his face looked better—yes, much better than it had in a while. Washed clean, somehow. If only he'd stop this silly business of putting on

other people's faces. It was so disconcerting—
she never knew from day to day who he was.

But what was this? Ula put a hand to her
heart. Sitting beside him on the ground was
the woman she had sat next to on the bus on
her way to the Castle, the one who had asked
her to look for Arietta. She could see clearly
now that she was, of course, her own grand-
daughter, her Silvia! What a surprising series
of events had united her with both grandchildren! Tears running down her face, Ula
rushed over to them, and Silvia, seeing that
her little grandmother was safe and sound,
burst into tears herself.

26

More than anything, Arietta wished she could fly home, rush right into the deli, and say, "I'm here!" She wished she could be there to help Belle with the baking of the bread, to run over to Luigi's for more milk, and at ten o'clock bring Sam a cup of coffee—but first she had a job to do.

She blew a kiss down to the deli as she flew over Mink and 21st, and then flew a little farther on. Soon she was right above the courtyard where she and Gus had tried so often to return. Below her a tall, gray-haired man was standing in a tee shirt and blue jeans collecting rose petals in a bag. Although this was not where she had intended to go, Arietta could not resist flying down. The brick wall was there today, rather than the hedge; but now, of course, for Arietta it was not an obstacle.

Arietta landed right next to Anton Van Lennep. He took a step backward and yelled, pressing a hand against his heart. But then as he took in the girl with her dark eyes peering out from beneath the hood of the artichoke cloak, he burst out laughing. "Why, that was marvelous, darling!" he shouted. "You took me completely by surprise, just dropping out of nowhere like that! I've been collecting rose petals for an evening gown and didn't see you coming! I must say, Arietta—you are Arietta of the Artichokes, don't think I don't know you, and don't think I didn't see you in my garden one moonlit night not so long ago—that cloak, if I do say so myself, is simply ravishing."

Arietta felt shy in the famous designer's presence. "Thank you for making the cloak. It's—it's so wonderful!" she stammered.

"Not at all," said Anton. "But come here, child, and let me take a look. I want to make sure the seams are holding up, and so forth."

Arietta wriggled out of the cloak, and Anton held it up so he could inspect it. "Hmmm, hmmm," he said. "I think it could use a little reinforcing here and there. Leave it with me, my dear. You may collect it at the next full moon."

Arietta, somewhat reluctant to part with the cloak, did, however, think it might be awkward to have it with her for where she needed to go next. As she handed it to Anton Van Lennep he waved a hand at the brick wall, and a door appeared. Arietta opened it and walked through, leaving the summery courtyard for the wintry street outside.

"See you in a few weeks, my dear. Ta ta," said Anton, and with another wave of his hand made the door vanish. Arietta stood for a moment beside the brick wall.

She thought about all the stories Ula had told her about the Flores family, and how, slowly, the names María and Pepe began to have meaning for her. María! That was the name of the woman whose magic mirror had been broken by Max. Pepe! He was the husband who had been so amazed by the magic working so well on Max.

The memory of that night came back vividly to Arietta as she stood on the very spot where she and Gus had stood behind a tree, watching the scene between María and Pepe and Max, almost as if it had been a play.

So, she thought, now she knew who María and Pepe were. Now she knew who the boy was they were looking for, and why. She even understood why María wanted to make a new magic mirror. Arietta raised her chin, determined now to go and speak to María and Pepe Flores.

She walked down the street and into the building she and Gus had watched Pepe and María enter. Just inside the lobby she found their names on a little strip of cardboard and pressed the button next to it.

"Yes?" a woman's voice floated out of a speaker in the wall above Arietta's head. Arietta stood on tiptoes and shouted, "My name is Arietta. Silvia is my godmother, and I'm friends with Héctor. Can I come up and see you?"

"A friend of Héctor's—?" the voice broke off in amazement. "Hold on, we'll buzz you right in. Come up in the elevator, third floor, we'll meet you at the door."

As Arietta stepped out of the elevator both María and Pepe rushed up to her, unable to disguise their eagerness and curiosity. "Our Silvia—she is your *madrina*?" María asked.

"And you know our Héctor, too?" Pepe asked.

"Yes, and Ula, too," Arietta said. There was a moment of awkward silence. "She has been living with Héctor for a few days now. She's very old and frail. Oscar died, and she has no one now. I think she is very glad to have found Héctor."

"*Sí, sí,* of course," María burst out, tears springing into her eyes. Pepe cleared his throat. He took Arietta by the arm. "You must come into our apartment, now, and tell us how you know Héctor. Silvia we see often, but Héctor disappeared some years ago. Do you really know where we can find him?"

Arietta was about to answer, but as Pepe opened the door to his apartment a large black dog came bounding out and almost knocked her over.

Pepe pointed a finger sternly at the dog. "Down, Max, down!"

María scolded. "Max! Where are your manners?"

Arietta stared at the dog—why, those puppy-dog eyes, that wide and jolly face— "Max," she said slowly, hardly believing her eyes, "looks familiar."

27

María led Arietta into the apartment. "Not long ago, our good friend Max looked into a new little mirror I made."

"It's magic," Pepe hastened to explain. "María designed it so if you look in it, you see the best in yourself. Can you imagine such a thing?" he asked.

Arietta nodded, thinking that someday she would tell them how she herself had looked into a fragment of such a mirror, and what a difference it had made to her, but now, she knew, was not the time.

"Arietta, not long ago I thought magic was silly." Pepe looked both sad and embarrassed as he made this confession.

María patted him consolingly on the arm. "Well, *mi amor,* those days are long gone now, aren't they? You've even learned a bit of magic yourself."

Pepe puffed himself up proudly. "Yes, I have."

"Tell Arietta about Max," María urged.

"Max was not too sure of himself—didn't think he could do much," said Pepe, thoughtfully gazing at the dog. Max gazed back, his eyes never leaving Pepe's face for one moment. "But when he looked into María's mirror, a brand-new one she had made, he said, 'I don't have a lot of real skills, but, you know, I'm friendly, loyal, fun, and enthusiastic. I think I'd like to be a dog.'"

"That's when Pepe took a course in transforming people into animals," said María.

Pepe shook his head. "It took me a while, believe me. Many, many hours, and after work, too. But then one day, *poof!* It was fantastic!"

As Max sat grinning, wagging his tail madly, Arietta couldn't help giving him a little pat on the head.

"Now," said María, "please, *please* tell us how we can find our boy. We want so much to see him."

"And Ula, too, of course," said Pepe quietly. "We will be more than happy to see her. And I only hope that she can forgive me."

At the Mink Street Deli, Belle was standing at the counter staring into space. Sam was sitting by the window pretending to read the newspaper. Arietta rushed in the door and threw herself into her father's arms.

Belle ran out from behind the counter, laughing and crying. Sam wrapped his arms around them both.

Pitter and Patter bobbled out of the back room. "Arietta of the Artichokes," they clucked, "you've come home."

The news traveled quickly down Mink Street, and soon the doors of the deli were open to one and all to celebrate Arietta's homecoming.

The Battle at the Castle made big news that day. Camera crews were out in force as the police finally were able to enter the premises without being attacked. Ambulances came and carried off the wounded.

The first bus in many days carrying castle-goers chugged up the hill and came to a stop. People streamed out, fascinated by the sight that greeted them. Mr. Mann raced up the ramp of the pigeon. In a few moments the audience on the grass clapped and cheered as the giant wooden pigeon's wings flapped and the eyes blinked.

Héctor, the cause of all the commotion, was nowhere to be found. While the public was distracted by Mr. Mann's demonstration of the marvelous mechanical pigeon, Silvia, Ula, Héctor, and Gus (released, after some heated discussion, by the orange cats) caught a bus downtown, and now they were all resting in Silvia's apartment.

It took several weeks for things to settle down. Sam and Belle had to make a statement they were not going to press charges against Héctor. They said it was all a terrible misunderstanding. The pigeons moved back to their former neighborhoods, and most of them avoided chocolate for the rest of their lives. Only Ruth stayed on at the Castle, and you can still see her there, marching back and forth in the upper courtyard, shouting orders at an invisible army.

The cats and squirrels returned to their own territories as well, and life went on as usual, the two clans not mixing much, as in the days before the Battle. But Frithby and Xiaolu had struck up a comradeship that was to become lasting. Often on an afternoon you can see them sitting by the pond in the park, one eye on the sailboat races, another on the chess players, discussing tactics and maneuvers.

28

And what of the Flores family?

On a moonlit night in February, a month after Arietta's tenth birthday, a long table was set up in a courtyard enclosed by a tall hedge. Outside on the street it was winter, but inside, trees were in full leaf and flowers bloomed. From the small house in the corner of the courtyard, the sound of a piano playing gentle dinner music drifted out into the warm, scented air.

Under the full moon the guests ate a delicious, creamy butternut squash soup concocted by Silvia. Sitting at one end of the table, Silvia kept stealing glances at her family, checking from time to time to make sure the soup was working. Sure enough, everyone who was invited, not just her family, seemed to be getting along. The conversation was loud and lively.

Ivan adored hearing about Ula's adventures in the aviary, and Héctor found himself talking more than he ever had in his life as Mr. Mann plied him with question after question about how to make bird houses.

Héctor, Silvia reflected, was quite handsome—and then she smiled. She'd not had such a kind thought about her brother in a long time. She did not know it, but only just that morning he had finally summoned the nerve to look into his mother's new magic mirror.

And what did he see when he looked into the glass? For once, an ugly image did not swim before his eyes. He did not even *see* his eyes—not even his nose or his eyebrows, his cheeks nor his chin. He saw a man surrounded by kids, a man he didn't recognize. "Who is that?" he asked out loud. "Who is laughing like that, and talking, and using his hands in such an animated way, and explaining things?" But then he thought, That's me. That's me at my best. He felt a tingling all along the top of his head as a new thought jumped into his mind: The best thing about me is how I am when I am with kids.

Héctor suddenly had a vision. He saw himself using the magic his grandfather had taught him when he was a little boy. He would shrink kids (with their parents' permission, of course) and horses and conduct miniature jousting tournaments in the big hall of the Castle. He would use his carpenter skills to build a miniature castle in the upper courtyard, and for one day kids could experience life in a castle.

Héctor did not know it yet, but he was destined to create the best medieval museum education program in the country.

Still looking around, Silvia saw that Belle and María and Mrs. Mann had discovered they all loved reading the same mysteries. They were discussing the plots in high, excited voices. Sam's deep laugh rang out as Pepe told him jokes. Gus and Arietta were amusing themselves by talking to each other in Cattish.

And smiling, Silvia noticed that, just for this occasion, Pitter and Patter had allowed Héctor to enlarge them so they wouldn't feel intimidated by the cats. Even so, they sat at one end of the table and tried not to seem rude as they cast nervous glances in the direction of Xiaolu and Uncle. The cats, however, were far too interested in talking to each other about mouse liver pâté to pay any attention to the birds at all. Pitter and Patter ended up having a wonderful evening as they shared old-lady-in-the-park stories with Frithby. Max sat happily under the table and begged for scraps.

And across the long expanse of tablecloth and rows of bowls filled with artichokes (for they, of course, were also on the menu), Anton Van Lennep, from where he sat at the other end, winked at Silvia, and Silvia felt her heart sing.

Sam and Belle provided the dessert—a creamy chocolate cake topped with raspberries and macaroons. Much to the delight of Pitter and Patter, Bird-Speak was served as an after-dinner tea. The pigeons enjoyed themselves even more as now they were able to speak to everyone.

But when the meal was finally over and the plates all washed and dried and put away—everyone helped, crowding into the kitchen of the little house—the guests sat back down at the table.

For a moment it was quiet, but then dance music filled the air of the summery courtyard. Cats of all sorts leaped under, over, and through the hedge. They danced the samba under the moon, and the guests at the table could not keep their own feet from tapping as they watched.

From where she sat, Arietta could just see the tail of the yellow cat as he played the piano, swishing, swishing in time to the music. Then as baroque music swirled into the air the cats formed two lines.

Uncle stepped forward and proffered a paw to Gus. Standing, Gus bowed, and then he joined the dance, as dignified and graceful as any cat.

Arietta of the Artichokes, wearing her cloak on this special occasion, looked into the hearts of all those around her, and smiled. Each heart was filled and happy, and so was hers.

$16.95

Connetquot Public Library
760 Ocean Avenue
Bohemia, New York   11716

GAYLORD S